Wishful Thinking

Wishful Thinking

Derek Corbett

Bridge House

British Library Cataloguing in Publication Data
A Record of this Publication is available from the British
Library

ISBN 978-1-907335-98-3

This edition published 2021 by Bridge House Publishing
Manchester, England

CONTENTS

INTRODUCTION

Being a Libra, I believe justice is important, as is love and hope. The stories in various ways reach more than one of these conclusions. Their endings however are not always legal but rely on an element of **WISHFUL THINKING**.

Derek Corbett

SNOWDROPS

Mary stood next to her husband, looking out the patio windows at their neat back garden.

"It's a shame that once those little red flowers on that bush have gone. There's no more colour in the garden until the crocuses sometime after Christmas," she complained. "Still the blooms may be gone, but they're not forgotten and anyway they come out next year to remind you."

Bert looked up at her from his NHS wheelchair and spoke slowly so as not to get out of breath. "I wish I knew more about flowers, then I'd be able to make sure you had colour the whole year round."

Mary bent down to tuck the big man's blanket in tighter around his knees and kissed his cheek. "You trying to chat me up, you big softy? Anyway, I'm happy with what we've got, our own wee house and the best garden in the street."

She didn't add that she would have given it all up just to see her man back on his feet. The price he'd paid working in the pit had been too high. If only he'd packed up ten years earlier. Knowing that to think about him getting any better would only bring tears, she added quickly. "Still at least after the first crocus there's colour."

Trying not to make it sound like an apology, which of course it did, Bert replied. "True, but knowing how much you like colour in the garden…"

His words faded as further conversation was brought to an end by one of his too frequent coughing fits. Mary left for the kitchen so as to try and not hear his suffering. There she busied herself making his lunch.

Bert was still looking out on to the garden when she returned to the sitting room. He turned his chair to face her. "Anyway, I've already put a plan into action for next year. With luck, you may at least get one of the things I know you wish for."

She moved his medicine to one side of the small table that always stood beside him and put down the sandwiches and thermos flask. "So, what's this plan?"

Rubbing his chest Bert gave her a weak smile. "Can't say at the moment. It may not work, but I wanted to let you know I tried. If it does work your crocuses will never be the first and only bloom again.

Mary brushed the stubble on his cheek affectionately with the back of her hand and smoothed his thinning hair. "You'll need to be back on your feet before you can do anything about any plans, so just concentrate on that for a start."

She gave the small table a final check and pointed at the sandwiches. "Now make sure you eat those. There's coffee in the flask and don't forget your medicine at three o'clock. The remote TV thingy is in this pocket on your chair. I won't be late but our Carol wants to get the boys their Christmas presents, so I'm picking them up from school and looking after them till she gets back."

"Off you go woman and stop fussing and give my love to them all. I might cut the grass if there's nothing on Telly."

Gently slapping the back of his head to cover her feelings, Mary took a quick look at his presentation clock standing on the mantelpiece. A reminder of all the early mornings and time spent underground. "That'll be the day," she laughed. "Anyway, Pet, got to go I'm running late." She gave him a peck on the cheek and hurried into the hall. She quickly slipped on her coat and opened the front door. "Won't be too long pet."

With so many of the family and friends present at the funeral, Mary was surprised how well it had gone. Even so, she was still glad when she heard the front door close behind her daughter and family, the last to leave. She'd been lucky, she reminded herself, at least Bert had lasted longer than some of the men in the village and it was a relief to know his suffering was over.

At Christmas, already getting used to being on her own, Mary was glad to leave her daughter's and get back to the peace and quiet of her own wee house with the best-looking garden in the street. And at New Year, having declined invitations from family and neighbours, she was content to sit in her armchair watching the celebrations on TV.

At midnight she toasted the presentation clock, now always addressed affectionally as Bert, and poured and drank a second port and lemon while continuing to watch until the last firework before taking herself to bed.

Next morning, the first of a new year, Mary drew back the curtains of the window that looked over the patio. She was greeted by bright sunshine and a lawn heavy with dew. Thoughts of her last conversation with Bert coming back, made her whisper, as if he was still there.

Well Bert that's a good bright start for the New Year, even if there isn't a bloom in sight.

As she was about to turn away a patch of white, standing out against the green at the far end of the lawn caught her attention. Her candlewick dressing gown pulled tightly around her she slid the patio door open. And with her eyes fixed on the white patch, she stepped out onto the patio in her slippers and shuffled across it onto the damp grass, not stopping until the white patch was there at her feet.

"Snowdrops," she exclaimed, "and not a crocus in sight. So, that's what the old romantic was planning."

Mary remained looking down at the small but perfect white flowers until a shiver reminded her that it might be the white flower's time, but winter was not a good time to stand around in damp slippers admiring them. She hurried indoors dabbing the tears from her cheeks and closed the patio door against the cold, wondering how he had managed to get the bulbs and plant them.

It wasn't until her two grandsons made their regular Sunday morning visit that the question was answered.

"Granddad sent us to the corner shop to get them and then told us how to bury them, but said it had to remain a secret until they were in bloom," explained Tommy the eldest.

"We planted them all on our own," added Jack his younger brother excitedly. "Told us to say…" Jack hesitated and looked questioningly at his older brother opening a sheet of paper.

"He told us to read you this. He said you would understand, Gran."

"Mary, I hope you can see the little white snowdrops even when it's time for the crocuses, but if you can't I know you'll remember them. Love Bert."

DOUBT

The faces of the six friars sitting around the table were serious and solemn. Every pair of eyes closed, the clasped fingers of their hands white and senseless from a night spent in prayer. Outside, the lonely sound of the towns church clock struck telling them it would soon be dawn. A bright flash of lightening illuminated the comfortably furnished room in which they sat and woke Brother Mercy, the oldest of them.

At the head of the table the prayer leader waited until the expected crash of thunder had faded before opening his eyes to look around the table.

"Well brothers, I think we have prayed long enough. The Master has not come in answer to our prayers, those of his earthly representatives. I believe therefore, that we have proved what we all perhaps have been thinking for some time. That the Master, whose path we have been attempting to persuade the townsfolk to follow, does not exist."

Sounds of movement came from around the table as hands were unclasped, eyes opened, and heads raised to look towards their prayer leader. Expressionless, he looked to his left and addressed the fleshy face just visible beneath the rough grey hood. "Brother Atonement what say you?"

The friar looked back with equally expressionless eyes. His lips hardly moving as he spoke. "I agree prayer leader."

The prayer leader turned to the next hooded figure around the table. "Brother Penance what say you?"

The corners of a mouth below a hawkish nose, showing the beginnings of a cruel smile, moved slightly as Brother Penance replied. "I agree."

Focused next on the boyish expression of the youngest friar at the opposite end of the table the leader asked, "Brother Doubt?"

The young friar looked back at the stern unforgiving

11

face of his prayer leader and hesitated a moment before replying. "I believe it would seem to be the case."

Moving quickly to look at the small middle-aged man next to Brother Doubt, he again asked, "Brother Confession?"

Brother Confession pushed his hood back from his forehead and looked thoughtfully around the table at his fellow friars before focusing on the leader. "I am afraid that I have no choice but to agree."

"And what is your decision Brother Mercy?" asked the prayer leader of the last hooded friar to his immediate right. "Are you convinced that the Master does not exist?"

The gentle-faced old man, his hood also pushed back exposing his grey hair and tired sad eyes, looked slowly around at the others and addressed them. "Despite what we and the brothers that have gone before us have done in the way of persuasion by the teaching and torture of the innocent in order to make them believe, I too am unable to continue in the belief that the Master exists."

Without acknowledging Brother Mercy's comments, the leader hesitated as another flash of lightening briefly lit the room. He waited for the distant rumble to fade before he announced, "Brothers I think that we can conclude that our night of prayer has proved beyond a doubt, that what the people believe in at present, is false and must therefore be replaced by a true belief. The people need our guidance, we must therefore decide what is to be done."

Brother Doubt raised his hand. "Do you have something in mind prayer leader?"

"I do not, brother. Before this night I had not dared to think that the Master did not exist and was not the true path."

"How will we find this truth?" asked Brother Atonement.

Brother Penance lifted his hand. "Is there no one we can ask?"

"The people, they may know what to believe in," suggested Brother Mercy.

The prayer leader tucked his hands in to the sleeves of his habit and responded, "How could they? They are not wise and all-knowing like us. They are just poor ignorant traders and farmers, incapable of choosing a Master to worship and a path down which to travel."

"How can you call them ignorant when they care for their families as well as feeding and providing a place of comfort and warmth for us?" asked Brother Mercy.

Brother Doubt raised his hand. "Is it possible that they could survive without us, but we could not survive without them?"

The prayer leader banged his hands down on the table in angry protest. "If they do not all believe in the same one true almighty, the one that provides all. They would each believe in something different. There would be chaos and mayhem among them."

The room fell silent for a few moments before Brother Doubt spoke again. "It sounds pretty quiet out there in the town at this very moment Brother; I hear no chaos or mayhem."

The prayer leader slammed his hands down on the table again. "And why should there be?"

Brother Confession spoke out in support of Brother Doubt. "Prayer leader, we have just decided that what we have been persuading the people to follow all these years is false. Does that not show that so long as they all believe in the same thing, be it true or false, there will be peace?"

The prayer leader opened his mouth to admonish the two brothers but was interrupted by Brother Atonement his lips stretched tight across yellow teeth. "What will happen to us if we don't find the true belief for them to believe in?"

"We will all become redundant, and they will rightly cast us aside," said Brother Confession.

13

"We must not allow that to happen," said the prayer leader.

"Then we must find someone, but not us, to blame when things go wrong." demanded Brother Atonement.

"Someone in whose name we can absolve them of their sins, before those sins become too heavy," said Brother Confession.

Brother Mercy raised his hand. "I must admit without us they would have no one to turn to for solace and comfort."

"Without belief there is no hope," said Brother Confession.

"There will still be doubt," observed Bother Doubt.

The room fell silent yet again as all turned to look at the prayer leader for an answer.

"There is only one answer," he said at last.

"What is that?" asked Brother Confession.

"We must pray."

"How wise," acknowledged Brother Atonement.

"How far seeing," agreed Brother Penance.

"Then let us do it immediately," said the prayer leader.

A rumble of thunder, now a long way off, sounded as they moved their hoods forward to cover their faces. Silently the brothers resumed the positions of the long night's vigil. Eyes closed, hands clasped, all were serious and solemn around the table.

"But to whom are we praying?" asked the gentle but firm voice of Brother Doubt.

WINDOWS

Bored out of her mind, Becky sat in her wheelchair on the small balcony of her tenth-floor flat and looked at the rows of windows of the other blocks forming the estate. It had been six months since the car accident that had made her life reliant on a wheelchair, lifts, ramps and the strength of her arms and shoulders

For twenty-eight years, as she kept reminding herself, she'd had a good life, football, dancing and plenty of boyfriends. Now confined to her flat in a wheelchair she was reduced to doing anything to pass the time. Like now for instance, counting all the windows that she could see in the three other blocks that formed the estate. Twelve floors in each block, twenty windows a floor. In all she calculated, scribbling the figures down on the piece of paper lying on her unfeeling leg, it came to 720 windows. Becky stared down at the piece of paper on her lap for a moment and screwed it up.

"So, what, who cares a damn?"

A clock in the distance struck two.

"Saturday," she mumbled. "Kick off time."

Becky thought a lot about her predicament. After all she had the time. What she had concluded wasn't that she was confined to the chair; there was nothing she could do about that. What bugged her was why she could not find the courage to leave the apartment on her own? For even though she felt imprisoned, she would do anything rather than face her fear of being outside her flat, unable get herself out of trouble.

She focussed again on the block opposite, and followed the reflection in the windows opposite of a white cloud passing overhead.

How was this for excitement?

15

"Oh, get a life or jump."

Her words, spoken out loud, were followed by a bitter laugh as she realised that jumping was not even an option. At best, all she was capable of was draping herself over the balcony rail, followed by a free fall. Realising what she had been considering, she hit her unfeeling knees with her fists. "What is your problem?" she demanded.

She concentrated so as to stop herself talking out loud and began to consider her situation.

Why was she so scared to go out on her own? It's not as if she'd get stuck on the ground floor. She'd done it all before when Dad had been with her. There's was even a specially built ramp for wheelchairs at the entrance to the flats.

Becky's argument with herself continued as she began to follow another cloud's reflection across the windows. A red flashing light from a ground floor window in the block opposite caught her attention. It took a couple of moments to realise that it was a torch and that someone appeared to be signalling her. Becky wheeled herself closer to the railings and continued to watch until the clouds reflection made the window go white, making the red light no longer visible.

Who was that? They were definitely pointing it in her direction?

When the cloud had moved on, she saw that the signalling had stopped.

Should she do something? It could be someone in trouble. She couldn't really call the police though. They'd think she was some kind of idiot. *"Excuse me officer I've seen this flashing light coming from a window."* The thought was suddenly replaced by another, more demanding one: she'd have to go herself.

"In this?" she exclaimed out loud, slapping the arms of her wheelchair.

All she'd got to do was go down in the lift, out of the building, through the garden and around to the front of that block opposite. She didn't even have to go in a lift when she got there; the flat was on the ground floor. So, what was the worst that could happen?

Becky wheeled herself back into the lounge, continuing to argue with herself.

She might get stuck somewhere... so she'd take her mobile. She'd fall out of the chair. Unlikely. Anyway, getting from the floor back into the chair is something she could do.

Not giving herself time to think, Becky put on her jacket, slipped her mobile and flat keys into her pocket and opened the front door. Outside in the corridor she took a deep breath and slammed the door behind her. The commitment was made now for the lift.

The journey, she admitted as she sat outside the front door of the ground floor apartment, had been one big anti-climax. There had been no struggling to reach the lift buttons, no getting trapped between the lift doors. So why had she been so concerned?

She leaned forward in her chair wondering if she was about to make a fool of herself and pressed the button. Unable to hear it ring or buzz inside, she pushed the button again. A man's voice from inside called out. "OK, OK I'm coming, don't panic."

The door opened to reveal a tall, well-built man with ginger hair, his hands, face, shirt front and jeans covered in what looked like flour. A big bright smile appeared on his face as her saw her. "Hi, how can I help?"

"I live in the block opposite on the other side of the garden." Becky hesitated a moment in case she didn't get the next bit right. "Now this may sound silly, but I saw a torch flashing from one of your windows, and I wondered if someone might be in trouble. But..." Becky paused and

17

pointed to the flour on his shirt. "I can see that you appear to have everything in hand, more or less."

"Ah, well, I am sort of having a problem, but not the sort that needs a flashing torch to rescue me. I'm baking, or trying to…"

Becky's smile broadened to a wide grin at the expression of frustration on his face. "I'll leave you in peace then," she offered turning her chair away from the door.

The man raised a hand, sticky with dough, to stop her. "Hang on a minute, please." The man turned his head and called, "Toby."

Slowly the door at the end of the hall opened and a small boy of about six, wearing camouflaged jacket, trousers and carrying a toy rifle, walked towards them.

"My son."

The boy's hair was almost the same colour as his father's. Becky began to laugh as the boy, his arm wrapped around his dad's leg, had his hair ruffled, depositing flour and dough onto it. He took hold of a torch dangling by a strap from his son's camouflage belt and held it up. "Have you been flashing this out of the window?"

The boy nodded enthusiastically and in a deep voice for such a young child explained. "I was signalling a helicopter to pick me up. The mission was complete."

"Well the pretty lady saw your signal and thought you were in trouble."

Toby shook his head. "No, the mission was successful."

Becky and the man looked at each other and began to laugh.

"I'm so sorry for dragging you round here but it looks like Rambo got a little carried away with his game."

"That's OK, it was nice to meet you both." Becky's cheeks began to redden a little at the admiring looks the man was giving her. She started to turn towards he door, but was suddenly stopped as the boy ran forward and grabbed the arm of her wheel chair.

"Can you make steak and kidney pie?"

"Can I make what?" Becky laughed.

His dad stepped forward to cover the boy's face lightly with his hand and pulled him back inside. "Toby, you can't go asking people to make you steak and kidney pie."

Now with white streaks across his face, Toby wriggled free and again grabbed the arm of her chair. "Can you make steak and kidney pie?"

Becky looked at the handsome face of the little boy, who was obviously not happy with his father's efforts. "Well, yes I can, can you?"

"No," he said shaking his head, "and neither can Daddy."

"I'm sorry," apologised the man a grin of embarrassment on his face. "He had dinner at a friend's house the other evening. The mother made steak and kidney pie. Since then he's gone on and on about it. Eventually I gave in and said that I would give it a go. Unfortunately, it's not in our one and only cook book. I know pastry is made with flour and water so I was trying to work a miracle." He hesitated a moment. "Since his mum's been gone, it's me or no one that does the cooking and I'm not always successful I'm afraid."

Toby, now with both arms leaning on the arm of her chair looked up at her pleadingly. "Would you make it for us?"

"Toby," exclaimed the man, "that's rude, you cannot go asking people to start cooking for us."

Becky stopped laughing and looked up at the embarrassment on his face. "I can show you if you wish."

"Brilliant," shouted the boy grabbing her hand and attempting to pull her towards the front door.

"Toby, now stop it," ordered the man, lifting him up.

"But the lady can make steak and kidney pie."

"I don't mind really," said Becky.

The man hesitated and looked at his son, silently pleading for him to say yes. Extending the fore finger of his free hand, the man wiped another streak of flour, down his son's nose and looked at Becky. "That's very kind of you, if you are sure." He hesitated. "You had better come in."

There was no mistaking the sound of relief in his voice as he put his son down, and gave him a playful tap on his bottom. "Go in and clear your toys to give the lady a clear passage, then wash your face."

The man stepped out of the door and offered his dough covered hand for a moment before withdrawing it.

"Sorry, the name's Jim by the way, and that was Toby." He pointed to the closed door at the other end of the hall through which the cheering boy had already disappeared.

Becky sensed that he wasn't sure whether he should push the chair or not so she began to wheel herself through the door way. "It's Becky and it's probably better if I drive."

"I really do appreciate this, perhaps you would join us for our steak and kidney. I'm sure I've bought too much. That's if you've nothing better to do."

Becky looked up at him and smiled. "No there's nothing I have to do, and it's a lot better than counting windows."

"How's that? asked Jim as he closed the front door?"

Becky began to propel herself optimistically down the hall. "I'll explain over the steak and kidney pie," she called over her shoulder.

DISASTER DAY

Right from the moment I woke I knew the day was going to be a disaster. The wind and rain were so bad it was definitely freakish, as bad as any I'd ever seen on TV. It was obvious not even keen fishing types like the 'Fish Finger Five' were going to brave those sorts of conditions.

The disaster didn't stop there either. It was to lead to even more significant individual disasters with far reaching repercussions to our entire village. A village, which up to that day had not possessed one bit of community spirit whatsoever.

We've always blamed Len for what transpired, he being in the chair for the 'FFF Club' that year. It had been his responsibility to phone around to confirm or not that the fishing was off. By the time he had got around to ringing Tom, the last on the list however, he was recommending an alternative competition to replace the cancelled fishing.

It was agreed that the judging for this one-time event would take place at noon in our local the Half Moon. It used to be called The Moon until a tanker losing its brakes on the hill outside, managed to knock down half the building. Although rebuilt the same size, the name Half Moon, meant initially as a joke, was adopted and a new sign was soon swinging over the door.

Turning up in time to witness Norm, the landlord, unlocking the door, we made our entrance to our usual bar each carrying a cardboard box containing our best effort. The boxes were placed on the bar with the correct amount of solemnity, the proper procedures were followed and a round was ordered. Later, with the tension relaxed a little, and a second pint standing next to each box, Len announced, "Right gentlemen it's time."

The lunch time regulars at other end of the bar sensing

that something momentous was about to happen, turned towards us, their conversation lowered to a whisper.

I truly believe that at that moment, even if any of us five had known the size of the disaster that was about to be revealed, none would have tried to withdraw or change the rules. But then that's the sort of blokes we are. Play the game as agreed and let the best man win.

Len placed his hands reverently on his box lid. "Gentlemen take up your positions."

Without a word we moved forward, placing both hands on our box lids.

"Remember its lids off, lift out your entries and place them on the bar. Then taking your box and pint with you take two steps back. There must be no last-minute adjustments and no one speaks until Norm announces the winner."

An expectant silence had now come over the regulars as if deep down in their primal psyche, they knew things were about to change forever.

"Lids off," ordered Len.

In unison, five lids were removed, five entries lifted out of their boxes and placed on the bar and five silent contestants picked up their empty box and pint to take the two paces back. The whole bar remained silent for what seemed an age. No one, it seemed even breathed. Then Jim the quiet one of the FFF but probably the most observant, spoke those memorable words that are still used today to describe exactly what stood on the bar.

"Disaster Day cakes."

There in full view of all those present, complete with topping, stood five collapsed shapeless almost unrecognisable cakes. It was at that moment it suddenly become very apparent to five of the finest freshwater fishermen in the district that cake-making was not the doddle we had all assumed it to be.

"How do I pick a winner out of that lot?" pleaded Norm.

A woman regular at the other end of the bar, who obviously did not understand the true meaning of that solemn moment, was heard to say, "With great difficulty."

Respectfully the petty comment was ignored and none of us five replied, but continued to gaze at our somewhat unworthy efforts.

"Taste," suggested Jim suddenly.

The same woman was heard to comment. "Taste?"

"Taste," repeated Jim, sticking to his guns. "After all, they can't be judged on structure or finish. They're hardly recognisable."

That very afternoon it was decided by the FFF that henceforth one day a year would be set aside for a cake-tasting competition. To take place twenty-one days after the Fish Finger Five's traditional fishing day celebration. Now five years later, the number of competitors has grown with nearly half the male population of the village, who are either married or over the age of twenty-one, taking part.

After the second year, two new rules were introduced by the committee to help maintain the spontaneity of the competition. Shop-bought mixes were banned and there must be no practice cake-making during the year by those entering. There has also been a competition introduced for those more interested in the techno features, such as structure and texture. This however is competed on a pub basis between the Half Moon and the Crown at the other end of the high street.

It is quite often asked why women do not take part in the Disaster Day cake competition. Strange though it may seem, to date no woman has expressed a desire to participate. Why, I have my own theory, but whatever happens in the future it is essential that the competition remains open only to those with a doubtful ability in the skill of cake-making.

By the way and rightly it was felt, Len was the winner of the very first Disaster Day cake competition.

THE BENCH

James Peter Stimpole, Jimmy to those that had known him before he had become eighteen and left the small quiet seaside town, dropped a large pebble over the cliff edge and started to count. The sound of it hitting the narrow rocky shore line made him nod his head with satisfaction and step back over the rail.

Back sitting on the old familiar wooden bench, he began to recall all the years away at sea. They had been good years, but had flown by too quickly. He'd hardly been aware of their passing. Suddenly age had stepped up behind him, laid a hand on his shoulder and whispered in his ear. He'd tried to ignore it but at sixty-five the company had beached him for good.

Back in his home town, where he had returned and then only because everywhere else, he'd ever docked had been temporary. He'd spent the last two years wandering the same old seaside streets, recognising the same bucket and spade stalls, ice cream signs and pink sticks of rock. The cliff top bench with its view of the sea and the far horizon had become the only place where he could escape with his memories and forget for a while the dull day to day existence he was now forced to live.

It was also here, on the plain wooden slatted bench, he would have to make his decision. To end it all or suffer yet more years of boredom and loneliness. To die would be the easy option; all it entailed was to stand up take the four maybe six paces, to the low rail, step over on to the strip of clifftop grass. Walk four more paces and then no more loneliness, boredom or sadness. The decision to live however was harder. For that he had to have a reason and at the moment he just didn't have one.

Unaware that below in the town the lights were slowly

going out, leaving only a few streetlights to greet the dawn, he continued to ponder the same old problem and recall how his life had panned out. Had he been a good person? Where had he failed, had he been fair to others? Selfishness, he concluded, had been his biggest failing. Even his mother, when he told her he was leaving, had called him a good son but a selfish one. Unfortunately, he had to agree, he would not score ten out of ten. Selfishness, doing his own thing, was definitely his main trait.

It was early morning cold that woke him. He knew then there wasn't going to be any sudden inspiration, no flash of light to show him an acceptable alternative. The time for thinking was over. He needed to take that last short walk before the first light of a new day appeared on the horizon to weaken his resolve. It had been like that at sea. As soon as he had seen dawn light up the horizon, there would be promises of all the new things to come. Now he knew that all it really promised was just more of the same: loneliness and the walking of those dull too familiar streets.

Determined, Jimmy put his hands on the bench and prepared to stand up on his cold stiff legs and take those last few steps. Something under his left hand however did not feel right, it was not the feel of a wooden bench.

What on earth...? He grasped the object. It was a book that must have been there all night and he hadn't even noticed it.

Jimmy looked at the title.

"Loves of a Lonely Poet."

Definitely not his type of read. When it came to poetry, he'd never progressed much beyond the brief but sometimes humorous lines on lavatory walls. Jimmy gave a chuckle as the thought occurred to him.

No point in starting it now; he'd be on the rocks before the end of the first line.

Jimmy opened the book and removed a plastic card marking the page. The sensitive words of the poem's first line drew him on to the second and the third, until it had all been read and tears were running down his cheeks.

Jim cuffed them away with the sleeve of his jacket, and tried to read the words again, but his vision kept blurring. He shut the book and looked up and out to sea. He was too late. The first glimmer of day was already on the horizon.

Jimmy continued to stare at the new day until the sea breeze had dried his eyes. He knew he would not be taking those last steps, not today anyway. Taking hold of the book mark and held it up to take advantage of the morning light, he saw that it was a bus pass. He studied the photograph. It was of a woman who looked homely and friendly; her grey curly hair was natural, her eyes had a calmness a... he searched for a better word... serenity about them.

The longer he looked at the photo, the more familiar the face became. But then he reasoned, all faces in the seaside town had become familiar. Even the name on the pass seemed familiar.

"Miss L Stoppard,"

Then it came to him. Lily! Lily Stoppard. Immediately the memories of the first summer after leaving school, came flooding back. Constantly together, from the moment of their first date until the final passionate 'Good bye'. There had, he recalled, been so much laughter.

Such a happy time he recalled. Unfortunately he had been too restless and too immature to know what being in love was really about. Eventually the need to see the world outside the small seaside town had been too great and he had left to sign on the first merchant ship that would take him.

They had of course exchanged letters of longing and undying love, but as he now knew, they had only been

27

words. Eventually, time and distance had weakened their young feelings for each other. He couldn't even remember who had stopped writing first. The photo however was definitely of Lily. Even with the passing of time he could tell she was his Miss L Stoppard.

"Miss," he uttered out loud. "Surely, she must have married?"

Had she perhaps come to the bench just to write and read poetry? Maybe she even looked out to sea and thought about him?

Jimmy started to laugh out loud, shaking his head in disbelief.

You big headed b... there you go again thinking that it's all about you. Well it doesn't work that way sonny Jim as you know only too well. People do their searching and waiting for their own reasons and it is not always just about you.

Jimmy carried on staring at her face, his heart somehow lighter; the need to sigh for a moment's relief, gone. Should he perhaps try and find her? It had been a long time, a very long time. She might not even remember him, let alone want to see him. Then he realised, that was it, that was his reason not to step over that rail. He would look for her... but how?

He could keep a watch on the bench in case she came back for the book, but that could take time. Now it seemed there was a reason not to waste time.

His legs stiff, Jimmy stood up and began to walk with purpose away from the bench, the book *Loves of a Lonely Poet* by Miss L Stoppard grasped firmly in his hand.

A LAST JOKE

Steve, aware of the uncanny silence, watched the flakes drift down to thicken the layer of snow already covering his back lawn. A few minutes ago, at midnight, Pete's widow Jan, despite her loss of a year ago, had toasted her husband's life. A life in which Steve had played a major role as they grew up together.

Not being around to say good bye when he'd died, Steve had lived with the guilt the whole year. There was also the downer that the forty-three years of friendship, mickey-taking and playing of practical jokes on each other, was no longer a part of his life. Now he just needed a few moments on his own, away from the party noise being made by relatives and friends.

Lost in his thoughts, Steve at first didn't notice the small cloud of white mist coming together in the middle of his snow-covered lawn. When he did, there was Pete, cheeky grin and uncombed hair, standing in front of him just as he remembered. Surprised but unafraid, Steve instinctively addressed him in the manner he had for almost all their adult life. "Where the bloody hell have you been, you wally?"

"Good to see you too, Steve."

"I've missed you, you know."

"Course I do, but you've got to let me go mate. This lot here," Pete indicated behind him with his thumb, "are getting a little impatient for me to go with them."

Looking to where he was pointing, Steve shook his head. "Sorry, mate. Can't see anything."

"Oh no I forgot, you're still alive so you're not supposed to. Anyway, what I've come to say is, just because I died it doesn't mean that you have to give up the ghost. Or perhaps in my case you should if you see what I mean?"

29

The small joke brought a smile to Steve's face. "I'm sorry I wasn't there for you when you…"

"Died," said Pete finishing his sentence. "Don't be daft you were there when I was alive that was far more important."

"I know mate, but it's still difficult."

"Sure, it is but you'll do it. Anyway, they've only let me come back to say goodbye, so I need to get going."

"Already?" said Steve.

"Afraid so, and I won't be able to come again neither. So, give my love to Jan and kids will you and thanks for looking after them?"

Steve watched as his friend's image began to fade but then suddenly reform.

"Almost forgot. There's a couple of blokes here that want to know what a one-man band is. Any ideas?"

"One-man band?" repeated Steve. "Of course, I do, and so do you. You must have seen at least two or three in your life time."

Steve stopped, realising that it was the first time he had accepted that Pete was no longer with him. "Sorry, mate."

"Don't be daft, I'm dead and that's it. Anyway, what about this one-man band?"

"We used to see them in the high street performing to the cinema queues. They always played more than one instrument at the time."

"How did they do that?"

"Well, the ones we've seen had a small bass drum on their back, with a stick tied to each elbow. On top of the drum there was sometimes a pair of symbols with a string down to one ankle. Another bloke we saw had the cymbals strapped between his knees so he could bang them together.

"Anything else?" urged Pete.

"Well, sometimes they'd also be playing a sax or

trumpet. One bloke I remember had an accordion and a mouth organ hanging from an old wire coat hanger jammed on his head."

"Oh yeah," said Pete, a heavy suspicious tone in his voice. "And just how did he go about playing all that lot at the same time?"

"He flapped his elbows, and knocked his knees together and of course worked the accordion he was playing."

Steve smiled at the familiar sight of Pete scratching his head, making his hair even more untidy, as he tried to picture the image.

"It must be very difficult?"

"It's all a question of co-ordination."

"I just can't even imagine him doing all that at the same time."

Steve, now fully involved in his description, began to enthusiastically march up and down the snow-covered lawn knocking his knees together, and flapping his elbows while playing an imaginary accordion. He was also making the sound of a badly played mouth Organ.

Pete watched for a few moments and then held up his hands to stop his mate.

"OK Steve. Thanks a lot, we've got the idea. You've been a big help."

Pointing at a spot behind Steve, Pete's image began to fade.

"By the way, say hello to the family and friends for me."

Steve turned and looked behind him. Everyone from the party was now standing outside in the garden with big grins on their faces. His whole performance, of what his wife would later describe as an imitation of a lame chicken with a mental disorder, had been witnessed by all the family and friends.

From behind him he heard the voice of Pete laughing and calling out, "How's that for a last good joke, plonker?"

It made him realise that the joke had been on him. Steve's head dropped and he shook it in disbelief as he began to laugh. A deep belly laugh, such as he had not enjoyed since Pete and he had last been together.

Unable to see his face but concerned by her husband's shaking movements, his wife hurried towards him. "Don't cry pet; it will all work out in the end."

Steve looked up still laughing and held out his arms to her. "I'm fine. I've just been caught by Pete, playing a last joke on me."

"Well from where we are standing, it must have been a really good one."

"You know what, that's exactly what Pete just said."

THE BAG LADY'S REVENGE

Alice dropped the large blue and white plastic laundry holder and supermarket carrier bag on to the top step of the Town hall entrance and sat down beside them with a sigh.

Thank God that cold wind had dropped. She hated it even more than the rain. It cut right through her even though she was wearing two sets of underwear.

Her frayed topcoat tucked around her knees, she pulled out a half blanket from the laundry bag and wrapped it around her legs. The spot by the column, she knew from experience, gave shelter from the wind and if the sky was not cloudy, it was a good place to catch the sun. The other advantage was that it overlooked a crossroad with traffic lights, zebra crossings and shops. It was a good spot to watch the world going about its business.

It had been a long time since she'd had a reason to go anywhere and envied the people having a front door to return to. She'd loved her wee house; it had been her own world, but only of course when he had not been around. It was only because the place had been hers alone until the pubs closed that she had stayed as long as she did. At times the waiting had been so bad it had been almost a relief when he did come through the door. At least then she would know by the sound of it closing what to expect.

It had been on her fortieth birthday. He'd come in drunk as usual, so drunk in fact he hadn't even wanted to take it out on her, which in itself had been a birthday present. It came to her the instant the front door slammed. She was going to leave, and start again somewhere else.

Although she had packed her case, ready to leave, it had still taken a year to pluck up the courage and in all that time his fists were building up her resolve, punch by punch.

She smiled sadly as she remembered the last time she'd

heard him come through the front door. He'd been early, thrown out the from the Oaks and not for the first time, for making a nuisance of himself. As expected, he needed someone to take his anger out on, and he knew just the person.

This time however she had been ready for him with Granddad's old police truncheon hidden under her apron. After the first blow, she could have laughed if she hadn't been so scared, he just hadn't known it was coming. Standing there he had remained, fist raised, as the look of drunken anger on his face changed to cross eyed surprise. She couldn't remember much after that, until after one of the blows to his head, his arms dropped to his sides and he fell forward on to the hall carpet.

Truncheon half raised, she had continued to stare down at him until her breathing had almost returned to normal. Wiping the handle with her apron she had laid it on the hall table. Then without thinking, she'd put on her coat, picked up her case and left without looking back, leaving the front door wide open.

From then on everything had become a dream, not the type she'd had in bed, but the type seen in the old black and white movies. Talking heads coming out from nowhere, mouthing words she could not hear, watching herself walking, but never seemingly getting anywhere.

They said she had been found behind the London Palladium, more dead than alive from malnutrition and hypothermia. How she had got there and why London she had no idea. She had never even visited the city on a day trip.

In the hospital bed she'd had time to think. That's when she'd decided not to tell the authorities the truth. She only stayed a short while at the hostel they transferred her to. The fear that he might find her had been too great. Now almost eighteen months later she was one of London's 'Bag Ladies', sleeping wherever she could find safety and a little warmth.

He'd survived. In fact, her neighbour had told her when she had made the phone call. He'd only been badly bruised, with no idea how it had happened. He'd also had no idea why his Alice had left.

The church clock across the road struck twelve noon. Alice folded the half blanket and returned it to the laundry bag. Then with a bag containing all her worldly possessions in each hand she carefully made her way down the steps to the pavement and walked slowly the short distance to the alley – a service alley that started behind the town hall, which would take her to the back entrance of the Pescatore restaurant, and with luck a free meal. The thought that it might be lasagne, her favourite, made her walk a little faster.

The sound of someone running behind her made her move instinctively from the middle of the cobbled alley and lean against the wall without looking back. She'd learned early on that it was best for people in her position, never intentionally or unintentionally, to show interest in others.

The sound of the footsteps getting slower as they got closer, she knew, was not a good sign. But to look back would only complicate the situation. She prepared for what she suspected would come.

A hand grabbed her arm and turned her slightly away from the wall. "You, I know you, I've seen you around. I want you to hold this for me till I come for it. Do it right and there's a couple of quid in it for yer. Do a runner and I'll fix yer good and proper, got it?"

The cruel rough voice of a young man made her turn back towards the wall without making a sound.

"Are you listening, you old bag, take this or else." She could tell he was nervous.

35

Alice moved her hand away so as not to accept the plastic carrier bag being forced upon her. The hand moving on to her shoulder spun her round and pushed her hard against the wall. She closed her eyes and turned her head so as not to see his face.

His voice high, almost in panic but still with menace, began again to make his demands. "Take it. I ain't got time to piss about. I'll be back for it and remember I know where to find you, now take it."

The smell of his breath and body odour made her feel sick as she dropped her own bags and accepted the one being forced into her hand. A police siren passing the end of the alley made him look back. Satisfied there was no immediate problem, he grabbed the lapels of Alice's coat and pulled her towards him.

"Remember, I'll be back for my bag so don't do anything silly, cos I'll find yer."

The force of his slap brought her head up with a jolt, causing her to look directly at his spotty unshaven face. Now angry, Alice became determined to remember every detail from the close-set eyes above the spotty skin of his sunken cheeks to his hawkish nose and brown discoloured teeth.

The black woollen hat, pulled low over his brow made his face appear very small, reminding her of a shrunken head she'd once seen in a National Geographical Magazine. His threats continued until in almost a scream he yelled, "You hear me?"

She stared back coldly without a sign of emotion, unlike him with his curled lip's and eyes full of fear. If only, she had Grandad's truncheon now. "You said you'd be back."

Still held hard against the wall she allowed herself to slowly slide down until she was sitting among the plastic bags. She glanced up in time to see him take a last look back towards the alley entrance before running off in the opposite direction.

Alice sat watching the hands in her lap shaking. It had been a long time since she had been that frightened.

Slowly the Sun crept along the brick wall of the alley, until finding her, its warmth brought a sense of calm as it penetrated her layers of clothing. Her hands stopped shaking, her eyelids dropped and she drifted out of the real world to where her troubles for the present were forgotten.

The sun continued to move on until once again in shadow, she shivered and woke. Alice struggled to her feet and leaned against the wall looking down at the bags until her head cleared a little. For some reason she couldn't help noticing how the red and blue pattern on his bag stood out so bright compared to the faded colouring on her own. She stooped and picked it up, a handle in each hand. "Well girl it's make your mind up time," she said out loud.

Although scared of what she might find, it had suddenly become important to know what it was that warranted her being bullied by the scared spotty-faced young man. She raised the bag to chest height, pulled the handles apart and looked inside. At first, although the contents looked familiar, she was unable to make out what it was she was looking at and closed it. A second look however brought immediate recognition, making her look nervously up and down the alley at the large service bins and stacked bags of rubbish. Alice took a deep breath and again peered into the full carrier bag.

There must be thousands here, she thought.

She closed it again and looked up at the sky. "It's certainly 'make your mind up' time," she said out loud.

Frightened that her words echoing off the walls may have been heard, she checked the alley again.

"It's always difficult making one's mind up I find."

A man's voice, distinguished but friendly, came from behind one of the larger service bins on the other side of the alley. The bag dropped from her hands as she instinctively covered her mouth to stifle the scream. There followed a moment of silence and then the sounds of someone climbing to their feet behind the bin across the alley.

Her heart again pounding, she remained silent as a middle-aged man with a big friendly grin on a sun-tanned face, stepped out from behind the bin. His silver-grey hair, a little too long to be fashionable, gave him a very distinguished appearance. She recognised him immediately and let out a big sigh of relief as he approached. He, like her, was dressed in well-worn clothes, chosen for cheapness and warmth.

"Good afternoon. Sorry did I startle you? I shouldn't have spoken out like that. By the way we have met. Well to be more precise we've seen each other about."

"Of course, I've seen you in the park."

"You were asleep when I came by just now so I stopped in the next room." The man grinned and pointed back towards the bin. "The alley is not exactly the best place to be on your own. Safety in numbers and all that. The name's Tom by the way." The man held out his hand, "It doesn't seem to matter too much about a surname in our circumstances, don't you think?"

Alice accepted his hand and shook it enthusiastically. "I'm Alice. Pleased to meet you. I've never given it much thought really, surnames that is. But I suppose you do have a point."

Tom shuffled his feet as if embarrassed. "Well I'll not bother you anymore and once again. Sorry I made you jump." Turning to leave he stopped. "I don't suppose you fancy a cup of tea?"

Alice looked into two of the softest brown eyes' she'd ever seen. "Tea?" she repeated, immediately realising she must have sounded like an idiot.

A broad grin spread across his face. "Yes, you know, in a cup, milk maybe sugar."

"I'd love one, but won't it be difficult to find a place that will let the two of us in. After all I'm not exactly dressed for the Ritz."

"It's somewhere much better than that. It's the Pescatore... back entrance of course."

"That's where I was going before..." she hesitated. "Before I was delayed."

He disappeared behind the large bin. "I'll just get my bag."

Instinctively, Alice began to straighten her hat and tuck the ends of her hair in, while at the same time pressing her lips together to make them red. Lipstick was a luxury she could hardly remember.

Tom reappeared with a large blue holdall hung over one shoulder and gave her another of his knee wobbling smiles, as he stood to one side pretending to hold a door open. "Shall we go?"

Alice gave a small curtsy, picked up the bags at her feet and stepped off the pavement on to the polished cobbles of the alleyway. "So, you use the Pescatore as well?" she said, as they passed the back fences of the shop yards.

"Yes, I've known the owner for years. Used to come as a regular, only it was the front door then."

Alice gave a little giggle; it was nice to meet someone who could laugh at their predicament, even if it was sad. "How long you been on the streets?" she asked.

Tom thought for moment before answering. "Not quite two years?"

"A bit longer then me then."

39

"What made you join the great unwashed Alice? That's unless you'd rather not say."

"No, it's alright. I was basically what you'd call a battered wife. He drank and got angry. I was the one he took it out on."

"So you left."

"One day I realised that I couldn't... no, make that I wouldn't, take it any longer."

"You just walked out?"

"Not before I'd thumped him a few times with my granddad's old police truncheon."

Tom laughed out loud. "That's great, good for you, too many bullies in the world anyway."

Alice held back as they came to a gate on which the name Pescatore was painted, allowing Tom to open it. A man in white shirt, black waistcoat and trousers, leaning against a wall smoking, recognised Tom as they entered and held out his hand to greet him like an old friend. Then he saw Alice and held out his hand again, exclaiming in a heavy Italian accent, "So, you know my friend Tom."

"Only since ten minutes ago. We happened to meet in the alley."

"The lady and I were wondering if we could scrounge a cup of tea Tony?"

"Tea?" questioned the expressive Italian as if he'd been insulted. "Why you not stay for dinner Tom? My restaurant not good enough?"

Tom and Alice looked at each other, but Tony, was already on his way back to kitchen before they could reply and was calling over his shoulder. "Make yourself comfortable and I'll organise something. You know the way Tom,"

"Thanks Tony, you're very kind."

He waved their thanks away, and as he entered the back

door he called back, "So, what's a little lasagne between friends?"

Tom lead the way to a shed in a corner of the yard and opened the door. "Our own private restaurant," he joked standing back to let Alice enter. "I'll jam the door open for a while. Let out some of the smell. They use it to smoke in when it's raining."

They placed their bags in a corner. The shed to Alice, despite the smell of tobacco at that moment, was the cosiest restaurant she had been in for a very long time.

She stroked the smooth shiny surface of the white plastic garden table as she sat down. Looking at Tom, she whispered wistfully, "One of my dreams."

"What is?"

"Having furniture like this in the corner of a garden, shaded by a tree, enjoying a bottle of chilled white wine while watching the evening shadows grow long. Don't suppose it will ever happen now though." She sighed.

"One can never tell," said Tom. "I would never have imagined I would one day be sleeping rough, but here I am. But, if luck can swing one way there's no reason why it can't swing the other; at least that's what I tell myself on a good day."

Alice noticed a hint of sadness escape on to his face as he fell silent, party to his own thoughts.

"What do you hope for?" she asked softly.

Another of his smiles was aimed directly at her as he replied. "Nothing grand really; to teach again, a small but comfortable house, a car, all the normal sort of things that most people want really."

"So, you were a teacher. I thought you spoke a bit posh." she teased.

"Posh." He laughed. "Is that how I speak?"

"Well not posh exactly, just nice. Where did you teach?"

"At the London University."

"A lecturer no less."

"Head of Department no less." He puffed out his chest and pretended to hook his thumbs behind non-existent braces.

"So, what happened?"

"I made the mistake of trusting a particular woman, one hundred percent. She used me for what she could get and where it would take her. Then dumped me for someone a lot richer and a lot further up the social scale. But, worst of all, she betrayed me at the same time."

"How? asked Alice sympathetically?

"It's a long-complicated story. Maybe one day when we're sitting in that garden of yours, I'll bore you with the details. Anyway, I sort of gave up, lost my job, my home… the lot." He paused. "It's only been quite recently that I realised she was never going to be satisfied with what I could provide. The signs had always been there. I just hadn't read them or… maybe didn't want to. Unfortunately, as you are no doubt aware once out, it's difficult to return to the more civilised way of living."

Tom paused, realising what he had said. "Sorry I wasn't implying that wife battering is a more civilised way of living."

Alice smiled sadly, realising how sensitive he was to the feelings of others. "I know."

The back door of the restaurant opened, and they watched a large man in checked trouser and T shirt, and carrying a tray, cross the yard towards them.

"Tony sends his compliments and said he would have delivered himself but a big party has just arrived. He hopes you enjoy the meal."

"Thanks Benny. It smells delicious," said Tom.

"Hey, if it wasn't for you, my Gina wouldn't have made it through college, so no problem."

As he was talking, Benny had placed a plate of lasagne, along with cutlery, a glass and napkin before both of them. The bottle of red wine, already open, he poured into each glass and paused for a moment to view the table before leaving. "Bon appetit."

Alice, a tear rolling down each cheek, looked at the setting before her not sure if she should really be there. Sensing rather than seeing Tom reach across the table, she felt him gently wipe each cheek with his napkin before picking up his glass and holding it out towards her. "Your health, Madam."

Alice seeing his raised glass, mentally shook herself and picked up her own to return the toast saying the only Italian word she knew, "Salute."

Other than referring to its flavour and quantity as they enjoyed the lasagne nothing was said. Tom, the first to finish, leaned back in his chair and continued to sip his wine until Alice, placing her spoon and fork on her plate, proclaimed, "Benny must make the best lasagne in the world."

Tom picked up the still half full bottle and topped up their glasses. "It's getting a bit dark I'll put the light on, if that's OK with you?"

"By all means."

The single overhead bulb on, Tom returned to his seat and picked up his glass. About to raise it to his lips, he stopped and leaned forward staring at Alice's face.

A little embarrassed at his attention she asked. "What's wrong. Have I got dirt on my nose or something?"

"I've just noticed. You have a bruised cheek, is it sore?"

Instinctively her hand rose to touch it. "Some yobbo decided he wanted me to remember something."

Tom placed his glass on the table a look of concern on his face. "He hit you?"

Alice nodded.

"Would you recognise him?"

Alice closed her eyes, and immediately she saw the shrunken head under the black woollen hat. "Oh! Yes, I'd know him."

"But why did he hit you?"

Alice glanced at the bag in the corner and then at the man before her. To tell or not to tell? Alice so much wanting to trust her instincts remained for a moment looking at him unable to decide. Would this apparently gentle person with whom she had just had a delightful if rather bizarre meal, suddenly change, if he knew about the money? It could leave her having to face the yobbo on her own, without the money.

"I'm sorry," said Tom suddenly. "If you'd rather not say. I shouldn't have asked."

Alice rose and without a word walked to where the bag lay and picked it up. To reassure herself it hadn't all been a bad dream, she took a peek inside and closed it again, before moving to stand beside Tom's chair. His empty plate pushed to one side, she placed the bag in front of him and returned to her seat. Tom continued to look at Alice as if waiting for a signal.

"He wanted me to hold that until he could come back for it. I think perhaps the law was after him. He was very jumpy, especially when he heard the police siren pass the end of the alley."

Tom eased the bag open with one hand and peered inside. His cheeks puffed out and he slowly blew out air. "Bloody Nora, there must be thousands." He took a sip of his wine. "When did this happen?"

"This afternoon, a little while before we met."

"Was he slim built, a bit taller than you, black woolly hat and padded jacket?"

Alice nodded again.

"Same bloke," said Tom.

"You know him?"

"No, but I saw him being arrested."

"When?"

"Five, ten minutes before I turned into the alley and found you asleep."

Alice lay back in her chair, a look of relief on her face. "So, he may not be coming back."

"Not if they charge him with stealing this little lot," he announced.

Alice smiled as she saw a big grin spread across Tom's face. "What are you smiling for?" she asked.

"I've just realised. I've been dining with a very wealthy lady and didn't even know it," he laughed.

"The lady is very flattered that you asked her."

Tom picked up the bottle to share the last of the wine.

"But what if they release him through lack of evidence and he does come looking for me?"

"You could move to another area, but if he did catch up with you, you could say you had been mugged. He might be able to understand that."

Alice sat silently for a while sipping her wine before pointing at the bag. "What do you think I should do with it?"

"What would you like to do with it?"

"I suppose I should take it to the police."

"That's one option and there may be a reward, but I asked: What would you like to do with it? Assuming of course he doesn't come back."

"What else could I do?"

"Well," said Tom after a few moments, "you could keep it."

Alice thought over what he'd just said, but the idea

began to frighten her. "He could tell the police about me holding the money for him."

"I doubt it; he's hardly going to report you. You see officer; I knocked this lady about to make sure she didn't do a runner with me money, which I'd just nicked. Then she tells me she got mugged."

Alice smiled at his attempt to mimic an East End accent. "I suppose you do have a point, but it's still not right. I'd be stealing and therefore no better than him."

"Alice, you'd always be better than him, no matter what you did." said Tom gently.

Embarrassed a little by the compliment, not so much by what he'd said but the way in which he had said it, she fell silent. It had just dawned on her that this nice, gentle, man, who she had known for less than an hour, was actually attracted to her. She had in fact been picked up, chatted up, and taken to dinner without realising it.

He'd invited her for a cup of tea not because he was lonely, but because he wanted to be with her. Could he really be interested in her? She wasn't exactly dressed fashionably; even her hair was a mess and as for her hat. That had been chosen for warmth not style. Definitely not her figure. That was hidden under layers of clothes, and even her legs were concealed by a long coat and shin high padded boots. Maybe it was her face. She couldn't remember the last time she'd dared to look back at herself in anything other than a shop window.

Alice remained in silence trying to understand why he should feel the way he did. The money, it must be the money, but then he hadn't known about it till just now.

Her train of thought was suddenly broken.

"Sorry, have I overstepped the mark?"

Alice focused on Tom sitting opposite her across the table. "Sorry what did you say?"

"I was asking, if I'd perhaps offended you by being a bit too forward."

"No, no, I'm just a little confused."

"Is it because I tried to pay you a compliment?"

"Well yes."

"I don't see why? We've seen each other around for some time now and you've always smiled back. I know under normal circumstances it would have been a lot easier but I am not under normal circumstances. I carry all I own around with me and I sleep rough. I just felt that if we could speak as friends whenever we met, it would perhaps bring a little comfort into our lives."

Tom paused to see if Alice wished to reply, but then continued before she could.

"I must admit if things were better for me, then perhaps I..." he let the silence express its own inference. "But they're not, so I'm sorry if I have upset you. It was not intended."

Tom looked questioningly into her eyes as she reached across the table to lay her hands on his.

"You should have used 'us' instead of 'I and me' in that nice little speech," she said calmly. "As you say, we are not under normal circumstances. And if things were better for us, then perhaps we..." Alice stopped speaking for a moment before adding, "And no, you haven't upset me."

Relieved at her reaction to his advances, Tom whispered, "I'm glad."

"But what are we going to do about it?" she asked.

"How do you mean?"

"Do you want to be just friends?"

Tom smiled and turned his hands over to hold hers. "I think, I would eventually like to be more than just friends, but I'm not always this pushy so I'd be more comfortable moving at your pace, so to speak."

"Good, because I'm going to need your help."

47

"To do what?" he asked.

"To use the money to get us off the streets."

"You intend to keep it then?"

Alice gave him a smile.

"It was your idea."

"Only if you're happy with it. After all, we might be able to find some other way out of our situation."

Alice shook her head slowly. "I'm nearly forty-two years old; I don't have the time or talent to resume a normal pleasant existence without some sort of edge. The money will give me that edge, but only if I have help."

"You're forty-two," exclaimed Tom.

Alice felt a flutter of panic. Surely, he wasn't younger than her and only looked older.

"How old are you then?"

Knowing full well what was on her mind, Tom hesitated before answering. "Don't be so old fashioned. Lots of older woman go with younger men these days. Anyway, I shall be, he paused again... forty-five tomorrow... that's if it's the twenty-second."

Alice slapped his hands and leaned back laughing. "I thought I'd got myself a toy boy there for a minute."

Both sat in silence for a few moments trying to accept how much their relationship had changed in such a short time. A serious expression appeared on Tom's face as he began to speak. "I think we have to start thinking practically for a while."

"Go on," prompted Alice.

"The money, it can help us but only if we are careful. People like us do not go marching into estate agents asking to view or rent properties. We have to be a little subtle in how we move up market."

"Perhaps we should first see how big the problem is?" said Alice pointing at the bag.

Prompted by her words, Tom thought for a moment. "We can't exactly do that here."

Another moment of silence followed before he continued.

"How's this for a plan? First we exchange our luggage for something a little more respectable."

"You mean get rid of my luxury laundry bag?" laughed Alice.

"Then and I hope this doesn't offend you, we buy some clothing to smarten ourselves up a little."

Alice nodded. "I know what you mean."

"Then if you agree, we book ourselves into the right kind of hotel where we can have some privacy to count your money."

"A Hilton?" suggested Alice.

"Something a little more down market I think, only when we know just how much is in that bag can we decide how much we can change our lives. Is that what you had in mind?"

"Exactly" she replied.

"You know we're taking a chance that we will get along with each other," he cautioned.

"I don't mind taking another risk on top of keeping the money if you don't."

Tom gave her hands a gentle squeeze. "I think it will be worth it."

The couple continued to talk about their escape from the streets for a little longer, before calling their thanks through the back door of the restaurant as they left to start putting their plan into action.

The sun was almost melting the tar on the roads as the smartly dressed middle aged couple holding hands entered the front door of the Piscatore restaurant. The owner greeted them and gently took the lady's arm to lead her to a table by the window.

As always performing with his usual Latin charm he asked, "Will this suit signora?"

It was the distinguished looking gentleman dressed in blazer and tan slacks with neatly trimmed grey hair who answered. "Thank you Tony, this will be fine."

Something about the voice made Tony really look at the man for the first time. His mouth dropped open in surprise as he recognised the customer.

"Tom?" It was a question more than a statement of recognition. "It is. Mamma Mia, where have you been hiding yourself these last couple of years? Why you never come and see me now?"

Slowly he took in Tom's smart but casual attire. "You look so well, your luck she must have changed a lot?"

"Everything is perfect now thanks Tony and a lot of it is down to you."

"To me, why you say to me?"

"The lasagne and wine you served us in the shed out back performed a near miracle."

"Oh! Yes, I remember, but what about the lady?" He turned towards Alice sitting at the table a big smile on her face.

"You've met already," said Tom.

Tony looked at his friend's companion carefully; slowly his face began to light up as he recognised her. "The bag lady with the beautiful eyes who likes Benny's lasagne" he exclaimed.

Alice rose to her feet and kissed him on the cheek whispering, "The very same."

"What has happened to you both?"

"We've had a lot of luck and found each other. It just couldn't be better," explained Tom.

"You are teaching again Tom."

"English at a school in Norfolk. Nice area, good neighbours."

"So, what are you doing down here?"

"We've come to sample some of Benny's lasagne and a bottle of your house red."

"It will be our pleasure."

Again, Tony grasped Tom's hand and shook it vigorously before disappearing through the kitchen door calling out loudly, "Two lasagne and a bottle of house red."

After a visit from Benny and a meal that brought back such happy memories, they sat finishing the last of the wine, casually looking out the window on to the street.

"It's him," whispered Alice suddenly.

Tom turned to follow her stare.

"Across the street, sitting on the pavement between those two shops."

Tom turned his head further around to where Alice was pointing.

"That's the chap who gave me the money to look after."

Cross-legged, his hand held in front of him staring down at the pavement sat a scruffy-looking figure who despite the heat, was still wearing the same black knitted hat and torn padded jacket.

"Are you sure?"

"It's him alright," confirmed Alice from between tight lips.

"Do you want to go over and thank him for his generosity?"

"Hmm," hummed Alice. Suddenly she stood up and grabbed her handbag. "Won't be a minute."

Intrigued Tom watched her cross the road and approach the beggar but stop before reaching him to search in her handbag and take out a piece of white paper and a Biro.

Quickly writing something she then opened her purse to remove what he could only guess was a coin. Both the paper and coin placed in the beggar's grubby open hand were immediately stuffed into his jacket pocket. He didn't look up, and his hand returned to its outstretched position.

Alice remained looking down at him for a moment, before strolling back to the restaurant. A smile of satisfaction on her face.

"What did you give him?" he asked.

"A pound."

"What about the piece of paper?"

Alice smiled.

"Just a note to thank him for the money and to let him know that the bruise on my cheek where he hit me had soon disappeared. I signed it the Bag Lady. I'm sure it must have really pissed him off knowing that I had disappeared with the money he stole. But when he finds that bit of paper it will be a hundred times worse, because he'll know just how much money he stole and that I'd found him and he never knew."

"Alice Crocker, you must be getting soft in your later years, but you can still be a very bad woman," joked Tom.

"Maybe I am getting soft, but given the opportunity, I would still have used a truncheon."

LAST PAYMENT

"Iris! Where are you? I need a drink of water, Iris!!"

George grabbed his walking stick that was lying on top of the bedclothes and continued to bang on the floor and call until exhausted. Tense with anger, his head dropped back on the pillow and he listened to the slow casual footsteps coming up the stairs and along the landing, until the bedroom door opened.

"You called dear?"

George raised his head to look at the pretty woman in her early forties, standing in the doorway. "I said I want water. You deaf or what?"

"Yes dear, I'll get some. Won't be long."

Unaware she was no longer there he added.

"And hurry up."

Frustrated at what he considered was a long wait, he again lifted his head as his wife returned, a glass of water in her hand. "You took your time."

"Did I dear?"

"Don't put it there. I won't be able to reach it."

"Won't you dear?"

Iris cleared a space on the table closer to the bed, and put the glass down.

"What you been doing in the other bedroom, banging around like an idiot?"

"I decided to start packing dear."

"Packing for what?"

"For my holiday."

"What holiday?"

"The one I'm going to take."

"When?"

"The end of the month."

"You can't go. I forbid it."

53

"Do you dear, that's a shame."

"What do you mean it's a shame?"

"It's a shame you can't do anything to stop me."

"You mean you're going on holiday even though I might die while you're away?"

"I hope not dear. The doctor said you shouldn't last that long. Actually, it's a cruise, a long one so I can't really cancel it. But don't worry if you do last longer than the end of the month; I've arranged everything just in case. After all doctors do get it wrong sometimes you know.

"Arranged what?"

"Oh, things, like carers to pop in a couple of times a day, but only until they're not needed. The doctor has also promised to call in occasionally. I've also arranged an undertaker in case he doesn't get it right."

"You hard-faced bitch, how long you going for?"

"The cruise is for just over two months; it should be nice visiting all the different places."

"What about my funeral? You'll miss it."

"I did think about that, but then I thought; well you won't know I'm not there, and let's face it, I didn't want to come home and find you dead in bed. Anyway, I do so hate wearing black even though it does suit me."

"How could you be such a hard bitch, not going to your own husband's funeral, after all the years we've been together?"

"Yes, twenty-five years next Tuesday, twenty-five years of being bullied, knocked around and verbally abused, while waiting on you hand and foot." Iris pulled a chair closer to the bed and crossed her legs. "What did you expect dear. I'd play the sobbing widow in black, being helped into the crematorium on some one's arm?"

"What do you mean crematorium; you know I want to be buried."

"Oh, you'll be buried or at least your ashes will be. I found that graves are so expensive these days so I bought a smaller plot, just big enough for your urn. I've also arranged for the undertaker to bury it for me while I'm away. It's surprising what you can arrange when you have money."

"You cruel, heartless bitch. How can you afford this cruise? Where did you get the money from? I suppose you've sold the house already?"

"Oh, no dear I haven't sold it, not yet. After all, I'll need somewhere to come back to and apparently by law while you are alive, I would need your signature. Knowing you as I do, I knew that would be a no go. But don't worry, you were so generous making your will in my favour, I'm quite prepared to wait a little longer."

"So, where did you get the money?"

"Before I tell you darling, is there anything you would like to tell me?"

"About what?"

"Well you must have something that perhaps you want to tell me."

"Tell you. Why should I want to tell you anything?"

"I just thought you might want to say sorry, maybe make an apology for being such a tyrant and bully over the years."

"Don't be so stupid."

"If you say so dear, I just thought that you might want to confess, you know, like a death bed confession."

"Death bed confession. What are you prattling on about woman?"

Iris waited until her husband ended one of his frequent coughing fits before replying. "Well for instance, maybe confess about the affair you started, two years after we got married."

George rolled his head to look at her, his mouth open, eyes glazed like a frightened rabbit to witness the sweet emotionless smile she was giving him.

"I saw you the first time you went out with her. In fact, I still had the bruising where you'd hit me for the fourth time. I even consoled her two years later, when she dumped you because of your bullying and need to control. We became good friends, so much so she's coming on the cruise with me. Isn't that nice?"

"Money," snarled George. "Where did you get the money?"

Although she could see he was exhausted and almost unable to move, Iris could still sense his violence, brought on by frustration, struggling to burst out. "Can't you guess dear; you've made plenty of monthly payments towards it over the years?"

"You don't mean..."

Iris uncrossed her legs and waited again for a coughing fit to stop. Using his hand to try and ease the tightness in his chest, George croaked breathlessly. "It was you I was paying all those years?"

"Yes, dear! All those payments you made as regular as clockwork, every month, for twenty-three years and I've saved everyone."

"You blackmailing bitch. You tricked me."

"Yes dear, I suppose I did, although I looked at it more as a way for you to say sorry for being such an obnoxious human being. It was quite sweet of you in a funny sort way and so out of character as well. Paying every month just so your wife wouldn't find out that you had been unfaithful or did you calculate that it would have cost you a lot more, and in one big lump sum, if we had divorced?" Iris paused, waiting for another coughing fit to stop. "It's probably the only kind thing other than the will, you've ever done for me, in fact for anyone I suspect. Just think about it, nearly twenty-three years at a hundred pound a month, that's very generous when you work it out. In some ways, I wish I'd asked for more, but then I didn't want to be greedy and as I was probably going to finish up with everything anyway. Assuming of course you died first that is." Iris leaned towards the bed. "Have you managed to work out what all those payments add up too yet?"

"You bitch," she heard him whisper. "How could you?"

Iris leaned even closer and began to whisper in his ear. "You made it easier every time you abused me, but just think George, at least you won't have to make any more payments. Now you are aware I know about the affair, you can stop."

VICTORIA AND FRED'S BIRTHDAY

No one other than his family and employers ever heard of Frederick George Barlow but then, there was no reason why they should. His only claim to fame you could say was being born at the same moment the British Nation began to celebrate the birth of one Alexandrina Victoria the only child of the Duke and Duchess of Kent at 4.15am on the 24th May 1819.

She would come to be known as the longest serving Monarch in the history of Britain. Fred, as he became to be known, would also be long serving. But where Victoria's service would be monitored and celebrated, Fred's activity would go unnoticed and remain secret, until he had passed away.

After attending the local school Fred left, not in a blaze of glory, but with enough certificates to make him worth being interviewed by potential employers. He was presented with the choice of becoming a coffin maker's apprentice, by Smithson's the local undertaker or becoming a bricklayer like his father; he chose the former.

Soon after at the age of fifteen in 1834, when taking up his apprenticeship, to the day he died, Fred became known as the man with the handcart. Always happy to stop for a chat when delivering the high-quality coffins, he became almost invisible, an accepted feature around the community.

By the time it was his tutor's turn to occupy one of his own coffins, Fred's workmanship had become admired, outshining all other coffin makers both locally and in the surrounding boroughs.

There was never any fifteen minutes of fame for Fred. Even the adverts in the local paper only ever referred to Smithson's fine quality coffins, never to the man with the skill to make them.

The truth would probably never have come out, if, in the year before Fred shared his sixty-fourth birthday with his Queen. The Smithson family business, realising that their loyal long serving employee could not go on for ever, hadn't taken on an apprentice.

A bright, inquisitive lad, Eric Peter Collins was quick to learn. Which was just as well, for his apprenticeship ended prematurely after only two years and twenty days when Fred, struck down by flu, took to his bed for the last time.

Left to finish off the two coffins in production, and in eager anticipation of taking over from Fred, Eric in his enthusiasm decided to tidy up the workshop. Which is when he found a list in Fred's neat handwriting concealed in one of the small model coffins, used as displays, to show customers what they would be getting for their money.

Fred's list showing in detail what he had been up to, was quickly handed to Mr Frank Bertram Smithson, grandson of the first Smithson, as if it were a hot potato. In short, it listed the names of those bodies who were currently sharing one of Fred's coffins with one of Smithson's own legitimate customers.

It was realised that this was something that would have dire consequences if made public, so Eric was sworn to silence and duly promoted before a hurried visit was made by Mr Smithson to his close friend, the police commissioner for the borough.

Low-key enquiries established that some of the dates on Fred's list matched those on the borough's police missing person's list. The two men became convinced that here were crimes that would result in years of investigation and paperwork for both parties. As the commissioner summed it up, when he and Mr Smithson left the Home Secretary's office four days later with an agreement to forget what they'd found, *"Just how do you go about digging up twenty-five coffins, reaching back forty odd years, to remove the bones of an uninvited guest, whose remains can only be identified by a name on a list? Just to put them into another coffin and rebury them at the borough's expense."*

Happy now that responsibility was no longer his and the company's reputation was safe, Smithson was able to continue as before with Eric Peter Collins in the position he had been so eager to make his own. Eventually those in the know came to the conclusion that the choice of who shared with whom had been restricted to those that had begun their last journey from the Smithson's own chapel of rest.

The question of how the extra body had been concealed for the final viewing was answered by digging up, in secret, the last of those on the list. Fred's skill, it seemed, had included the ability to install a false bottom in the coffin. For reasons of prudence it was also decided not to question the bearers about the extra weight they had carried.

Assumed by those in the know that it was very unlikely that Fred was the one that had ended the life of the victims, and that he was merely concealing a crime by others for reward, left only two major questions.

Who paid Fred to make them disappear? And secondly, why had no one ever asked what lay under the covers on his cart as he walked about the community? Now that he was dead there never would be answers so the files were duly closed and lost in the archives.

And so, the Victorian era came to an end on the 24th January 1901, sixteen years after Fred died.

Both the Queen and Fred had spent most of their life in the full view of the public. But it seemed while she had struggled against the unseen officials around her, to live life as she wanted, he had lived a life that he had wanted, unseen among those around him.

The commissioner died seven years after Victoria. Mr Smithson died in the first year of the Great War. Eric, due to a gammy leg and his skill, remained as the coffin maker, eventually buying out the Smithson family business.

So, the deeds of Frederick George Barlow remain buried somewhere in the archives and may never see the light of day. The current owner of Smithson Undertakers, Eric Peter Collins, grandson of the coffin maker who found Fred's list, is still making and supplying coffins of the best quality.

It is not by chance therefore that for a customer requiring an occasional body to disappear, a resting place can still be found and as in Fred's time the sharing with a legitimate occupier will still only require a one-off payment, VAT free of course.

PROMISES

Jim shuffled behind his wife, along with the rest of the package holiday passengers and watched her step out on to the small platform at the top of the stairs to look out across the airfield towards the terminal building.

He knew what Effie was thinking. Why shouldn't he? After all his thoughts were similar. He too could still remember the feelings on their wedding day as they'd emerged from the registry office into the cold bright sunlight, convinced that their dreams of a home and a family were about to become a reality. With his apprenticeship in the local ship yards, it was to be a new start for both of them, after a life of unhappiness and poverty experienced when growing up.

He knew they would never be rich and he realised that he wasn't particularly toe-curlingly sexy, but he was convinced she loved him and that was all that mattered.

Effie put on her floppy brimmed hat as protection against the sun, hoisted the strap of her bag on to her bare shoulder and began the descent down on to the Greek island that was to be their holiday home for the next two weeks.

As she took her place on the small platform, Jim watched her tight brown curls bounce as she walked. He remembered sadly how those dreams had soon turned to nightmares. First the lifetime job in the yard had gone, then the small terraced house, with its mortgage had to be replaced by a dingy rented flat. From then on unemployment and underpaid jobs followed at regular intervals.

He had so wanted to keep the promises he'd made to the young lass he adored: a house of her own, a family. Their most uplifting moment in all their married life had been the move from the flat to a council house. Even their plan for a family had turned out to be a non-starter. His fault again. His tests had proved that.

He still loved her as much as any man could love a woman but his feeling of guilt had become all absorbing, and over time he had withdrawn from their relationship in shame. They shared the same space, but not each other.

The last three years as a taxi driver had made things a little easier, and the fact that they were actually on holiday abroad made him feel that for the first time he had achieved at least one of his promises. Taking the first step quickly so the tears he could feel welling up would not embarrass him in front of the other passengers, he followed Effie down to the tarmac.

Within the hour they had been delivered and were unpacking, in their opinion, in the most beautiful bedroom in the most beautiful hotel ever built. But then, this was the first hotel they had ever been in.

That evening, approaching the waiter at the entrance to the dining room, Jim mumbled a request for a table and chose a red for their all-inclusive bottle of wine. The couple sat at their table, attempting to show an air of confidence, for, despite the socialising hurdles in the imposing surroundings, they were determined to enjoy themselves.

After dinner, they found their way to the bar and selected a corner from which to watch the other holidaymakers getting to know each other, while making their free drinks last until it was time to leave. Effie was surprised by Jim taking hold of her hand to lead her between the tables. She was further surprised when outside on their way back to the room he suggested a slow stroll in the moonlight around the swimming pool.

Three days later, their holding of hands now instinctive, the only reason they chose the pale blue forty-foot boat with inside and outside seating for a day trip was because of the loud but friendly Londoner from their hotel. He had stopped to read the same chalked black board as themselves and had virtually shanghaied them into joining him and his quiet but friendly wife.

With no time to object, the unassuming couple found themselves sitting alongside the chatty Londoners as their boat headed out of the harbour, under the hot mid-morning sun. Later, moored in a small bay for lunch and a swim, it had been Effie's turn to surprise, by daring to slip out of her summer frock to reveal a neat little figure and an even neater swimming costume. She joined Jim in the clear warm water to laugh and play, enjoying a closeness they had not shared for long time.

On their way back around the coast after a long rememberable day of wine, beach and barbecue, the tired but happy revellers were suddenly silenced when a loud bang from the bow shook the boat. A timber, the size of a railway sleeper, had smashed a hole in the fibreglass hull. Very quickly the engine compartment became flooded and with the source of power gone, the boat could only wallow alone in the empty sea.

Though the crew and quickly sobering passengers managed to reduce the rate at which the hull was filling, it was evident to all those forming the bailing parties that they were only delaying the inevitable by a few hours.

Jim stood at the rail looking towards the island's shore line, thinking of his one remaining achievement that still gave him a small feeling of worth. When all other aspirations and dreams had failed, he had retained just that one thing. At forty-five he could still swim over a mile without tiring. All the years, when hope had been just a word, he had maintained his regular visits to the local swimming pool. Here, for a short time, he had been able to escape the day-to-day existence he had been forced to endure.

When he returned from his stint with the bailing team, Effie asked him. "How long before we're rescued Jim?"

"I don't know. The Londoner reckons the radio's not working, and it's unlikely the boat will be missed till the other skippers go down to the quay in the morning."

Further discussion was interrupted by the raised voice of the Londoner sounding even louder in the now failing light. "Well you're just going to have to swim to shore and get help."

It was obvious from the lack of response to those sitting around the otherwise silent boat however that the captain and his crew were either unwilling or incapable of making any such attempt. Jim looked around at the subdued passengers noting the closeness with which mothers were now holding their children. He slipped off his dark blue canvas shoes and handed them to Effie. "I'll have to swim for help."

Effie grabbed his arm and pulled him down to sit on the bench beside her. "It's too far Jim, we can only just see the shore lights."

"I've got as much chance as the others, maybe more, and perhaps this time I'll not fail."

"What do you mean, *this time*?"

Jim hesitated, reluctant to reply. "Well, let's face it. I've not exactly succeeded at too many things in my life," he said at last.

"That's not been your fault, it's just the way things happened."

"I wish I could see it that way. Do you realise that in all the years we've been married, I've only managed to keep one promise and that's this holiday... and just look at the trouble it's got us in to?"

Effie pointed towards the bow. "Jim Pollard, you're surely not blaming yourself for that hole in the boat?"

"Might as well, the house, kids, they were all my fault."

Shocked to hear her voice raised in anger, Jim made no attempt to interrupt as she grabbed the back of his hands.

"Don't be stupid. You have kept your promises. What about all those you made at our wedding."

"They don't count; everyone say's them."

"But not everyone keeps them," retorted Effie.

Jim looked over her shoulder at a woman holding her little girl close, tears running down her cheeks. Turning his hands over, he took hold of Effie's. "You've got to let me try."

Jim watched in silence as his wife stood up and walked to the handrail to look out across the dark calm water towards the shoreline and the twinkling lights. He could only guess what she was thinking.

Could he make it? What would he do if she made him stay?

Jim however, thought about the small changes that had occurred because they had actually been able to afford the holiday. He hoped that if he did succeed, it just might change him even more, perhaps give him the confidence he lacked. It might even give him the courage to allow him to approach Effie again.

The exhausted men and woman who had finished their shift at bailing, began to make their way back to their loved ones, too old or too young to bail. Jim, feeling Effie standing beside him looked up.

"Jim so many times in the past I've seen the sadness in your eyes but never knew why, and you would never tell me. Now I think I know why; I also think I know what is required to get you back." Effie hesitated and stroked his cheek. "So, you'd better go while you can still see the shoreline. But remember, when we see each other again, there's going to be some bloody serious talking."

Jim, having never heard her swear before blinked and whispered, "I promise."

Effie hadn't finished, taking hold of his hands again she sat down beside him. "But remember. I need a man in my life not a lodger in my house and that's you. Now get in that water and swim."

Jim pulled her towards him, and kissed her gently on the forehead. "Shan't be long love, just a wee while."

Those around them that had heard them talking, watched in silence as Jim walked away and spoke to the Captain. Even the Londoner remained quiet as he climbed onto the rail, and dived into the dark water. Approaching the handrail, Effie watched her husband swimming further and further away until even the dull florescence from the water he disturbed could no longer be seen. Still she remained looking into the darkness imagining each stroke he made taking him, she hoped, nearer to the safety of the shore.

It was nearly three hours before the lights of the rescue boats could be seen approaching. Once alongside, the passengers their feet now permanently under water, remained seated until called on by the Londoner to make their way to the point of transfer.

Effie, one of the last to be called, made her way towards the handrail to the sound of clapping. Reaching down to grab her hands, Jim helped her aboard and led her towards the stern to sit in the empty last row. Already he could feel his confidence returning, allowing him to approach the woman he had married. Arms around her he pulled her close and kissed on the lips.

Slowly the rescue launch edged away from the partly submerge vessel as another took it in tow for the slow haul back to the harbour.

The remainder of their holiday bore no resemblance to the period gone before. Now the other guests knowing who Jim was and what he had done, went out of their way to talk to them.

At night with the warm gentle breeze coming in the open balcony window they lay in each other's arms under just a sheet talking away, bit by bit, the years of lonely sadness.

Holiday over, still looking like their passport photographs, and still holding hands, the tanned couple disembarked at Newcastle airport with a renewed relationship and a strong feeling that this time they would win.

GLADYS'S TIME

CHAPTER 1

The removal man placed the box in the middle of the living room floor.

"That's its missus, no more on the van," he rasped, his voice hoarse from years of heavy lifting.

Relieved at being out of debt and finally in a place she hoped she could just afford, Gladys handed him a ten-pound note.

"Ta. 'Ere, buy yourself and your mate a drink."

Gladys removed her coat and hung it on the back of door. She strolled to the two well-used, floral patterned armchairs. They weren't yet in their final position, but she sat in the nearest one with a sigh, her handbag still on her left arm since saying good bye to what had been her mortgaged ex-council house that morning. She took out her dead husband's, highly polished tobacco tin, rubbed it a couple of times on her skirt for luck and reluctantly began the as yet, unmastered task of rolling her own.

Time and time again the paper failed to wrap neatly around the strands of tobacco until in frustration she dropped the makings back in the tin, replaced the lid and returned it to her handbag.

"Sod it."

Exhausted Gladys laid back in the chair and allowed her eyes to wander over her furniture and boxes spread around the room. They continued aimlessly onto the pale coloured wallpaper and up to the off-white ceiling, before finally settling on the oh-so-boring tiled fireplace. Tears, part from sadness part from relief the move was over, began to roll down both cheeks.

"Well Gladys, your forty-five with twenty odd years of marriage and this is what it's all come down too."

Her granny's old brown wooden clock standing on the floor by the kitchen door chimed two.

"Oh Alf," she mumbled.

No tears left, Gladys dabbed her eyes with her last unused tissue and shivered on feeling the sudden coldness of the unfriendly room.

"Well girl, you can at least stop yourself freezing to death, put the bloody fire on."

She eased herself out of the chair, lit the gas fire and crossed the room to stand in front of the curtainless window.

"Now which box did I put them in. I just hope they'll fit?"

By the time Gran's clock chimed six, and it had been moved on to the built-in cupboard to the right of the fireplace. The curtains, actually the right length and width, were up and making the room feel a little cosier.

One box, the biggest, remained unopened in the centre of the room where the moving men had left it. Others, now open and in various stages of being unpacked, stood in the kitchen and bedroom as appropriate. Gladys paused for a moment, then again looked around the sitting room at her 'bits and bobs' now beginning to find a home. Somehow even the wall lamps in the recesses which she had hated almost as much as the fireplace, now lit, didn't seem so bad.

"A nice cuppa I think, then make the bed."

In the kitchen, the kettle quickly found and the tap run for a moment, she filled it and placed it on the gas ring. The thought that at least the gas man had turned up to connect the oven on time brought her a little cheer.

But then he had been Alf's mate.

"Milk," she exclaimed out loud.

Gladys dropped the matches on the table and returned to the sitting room, put on her coat and grabbed her handbag. She checked that the keys to the flat and the downstairs front door were in her handbag and let herself out into the hall.

Faced with the door of the flat opposite, she hesitated listening to sounds of classical music coming from a radio inside. Nervous at disturbing a stranger, plucking up the courage, she rang the bell and waited for the door to be opened.

"Excuse me, I've just moved in opposite and I wonder if you could tell me if there's a local shop, that's still open at this time?"

The smartly dressed woman, holding out her hand greeted her warmly.

"So, you are my new neighbour. How do you do? My name's Helen, Helen Pollard."

Estimating that like herself she was probably in her forties, Gladys took her hand and tried hard not to let her lack of confidence sound in her voice. "Gladys Fenton. Pleased to meet you."

She always felt the same when meeting someone new and with real surety in them self, especially when dressed smartly like her neighbour. For two pins, she would have apologised for disturbing her and been off to search for the shop herself.

"Come in, I'll put the kettle on. You've got plenty of time before the shop shuts. It's only around the corner. It's one of those 'Seven to Eleven' stores, quite handy really."

Before she could even think of objecting, Gladys's found herself ushered into the flat and sat in a chair before a gas fire, similar to her own.

"Make yourself comfortable," Helen called as she disappeared into the kitchen.

The brightly coloured designer patterned curtains and armchairs, although welcoming, suggested money.

71

"You have a lovely place did you do it all yourself?"

Helen returned from the kitchen and sat opposite Gladys, unconsciously stroking the arm of the chair. "Thank you, yes it's surprising what you can achieve when you can no longer afford to have it done and have nothing but time to spend. I can even brag that I did these myself, me who had never sewn a button on, until I moved in here."

"Aren't you clever? My place is so cold and dull, especially after the nice little house I've had to leave. It was only a two-bedroom semi, but we'd got it more or less the way we wanted it." Gladys could feel the tears beginning to well up.

"Don't get upset dear, I'm sure you will soon have the flat the way you want it. Do you take cream and sugar with your coffee?" Rising from her chair, she again headed for the kitchen.

"I'd prefer milk and one sugar if that's alright." Gladys dabbed each eye with a screwed-up tissue from her coat pocket, and watched her host return to place a neatly laid tray on the highly polished coffee table.

"Help yourself to biscuits. Was it husband trouble?"

"Well sort of."

"You're not alone there; I'm in the proceeds of getting a divorce myself."

"Oh, no it wasn't a divorce. We were pretty lucky in that way. No, he died. Worked for the Gas Board most of his life, out in all weathers. Then they privatised and made him redundant. Eight months later he was dead. That's when I found out he'd taken out a second mortgage a couple of years earlier to get our son out of some sort of trouble. Unluckily for me, the insurance that pays off the outstanding mortgage should you die had somehow been forgotten." Gladys could hardly believe she was spilling out her story so readily to someone she had only just met. She hesitated as the feeling of terror she had felt at the time came flooding back. "Well, with only the reduced widow's pension from the Gas Board, which isn't enough to buy a rabbit's cage let alone keep up mortgage payments, the place eventually got repossessed. Now I'm in a rented one bedroom flat and still going to find it hard to make ends meet."

Helen felt sorry for the woman who from her appearance, had not had it easy even when her man had been alive. She handed Gladys her coffee. "Can't your son help?"

"Help?" Gladys sneered. "He's that useless he can't even help himself. The only time I see him is when he wants something."

"I'm sorry; maybe when you've settled in it won't seem so bad."

"It's my own fault really. All our married life I'd left everything to do with money to Alf. Even with Kevin, that's my son, I was too soft. Alf tried to tell me, but did I listen? No! Mothers know best, ha! That's a joke." Gladys fell silent looking down at the cup in her hands.

"I never had any kids, not even sure that I really wanted any to tell the truth. Plus, he was a wee bit older than me. Anyway, just after we were married, he changed jobs, did really well. Always away chasing the next order and getting it, or so it seemed. Made company Director, then it's the big house, big car, trips abroad and so on.

"Then suddenly, I'm the out of date model and he's on to one dolly bird after another, all with the right attitude and skirt to match. I managed to get out with something to cushion inflation and loneliness while the divorce goes through, but it takes a long time. One of the annoying points about it all, is that you're supposed to manage on your estranged husband's generosity, until its finalised. Well, you can guess how generous he's feeling knowing that eventually, I'll be getting what is mine legally. Anyway, a couple more months and it should all be over."

Gladys, looked at the coffee table, not sure whether she should place the empty cup and saucer on it. "Do you miss him?"

Helen paused for a moment before answering. "Him? No, not now. The life style and other men's company, only as friends mind you, yes, I do miss that. But unfortunately, you find that once you are on your own, socialising with old friends, especially married friends becomes a bit awkward. It seems to put them under pressure to do all the inviting. Eventually it makes you begin to feel guilty. So, you tend to decline more and more invitations."

Gladys watched Helen place her own cup and saucer on the table before continuing. "Then of course, some of the wives are a little concerned that perhaps you may make a play for their men. From my limited experience, however, it's more likely that their men, may feel a little too keen to console you." Helen took the cup and saucer from Gladys. "I have a saying. The company of a man can be a real tonic but to marry one can be poison. You've got to have your own independence, whether married or not, and if you are alone it's nice to have your own bolt hole. Somewhere like this where you can close the door and say to the rest of the world, up yours. Unfortunately to enjoy all these things one needs money. Freedom can be sweet but it costs."

Gladys, only recently from her own small terraced council house, where she had always played the little wife with her view of the outside world by kind permission of TV and the Sun newspaper, watched Helen refilling the cups. She had never heard anyone speak in this fashion before. Even so, she somehow felt that she would ultimately agree with her, when she did think it through. But as for her ever

74

being able shut her door and say, "up yours" to the world she felt would be more a case of "please stay out," at least for a while. Timidly Gladys asked, "Do you have any men friends now?"

"A couple, but nothing serious. In fact, I believe that they enjoy their freedom just as much as I enjoy mine."

"You don't sound very bitter about what's happened."

Helen smiled. "Maybe I don't, but I am. I've had to learn the hard way what's best for me, and all because he liked something young and eye-catching on his arm and couldn't keep his canary in its cage. I've learnt that being bitchy about the little shit, when he's not around, tends to waste one's energy. That's not to say I would stop for him, if I caught him on a Zebra crossing. I think what I've learned is, not to hanker after revenge, but just wait until the opportunity presents its self. Then do it properly, straight between the eyes."

Gladys couldn't help smiling at Helens words, even though they were so forthright and alien to anything she felt. "What about the 'new model', how do you feel about her?"

"Since I sat the last one on her arse with a Tyson special, I almost feel sorry for any poor bitch that gets lumbered with him."

Gladys hand went up to her mouth in shock. "You actually hit her?"

"You bet I did, straight on the nose, blood everywhere, right in the middle of his office with his work colleges looking on. It was her own fault, arrogant little tart. She would have been quite safe, but no she had to open her mouth and 'whamo', I hit her."

"Gawd, I would never have had the guts to do that."

"In the right situation you'd be surprised what you'd do." Helen chuckled. "Do you know what was the most gratifying bit… after seeing her sitting on the floor? blood dripping on to her virgin white blouse, that is?"

Gladys shook her head. "I can't imagine."

"It was the round of applause I got from his staff, both men and women, as I marched out of there with my nose in the air."

"Never."

"It was a strange feeling, that although my world had just fallen apart, and my hand was hurting like hell, it was the best I'd felt since I'd first began to suspect he was two-timing."

"Fancy punching her like that though."

"Well, she had made me as mad as hell. I suppose really it should have been him, but as it wouldn't have been so effective. She, as they say, drew the short straw."

Gladys placed her empty cup and saucer on the coffee table alongside Helen's.

"I wish I could do something like that, instead of feeling as though I'm the one being knocked from pillar to post. First by the Gas Board, then by the mortgage people and lastly by that creep of a son."

"Don't worry, your turn will come. Just you wait and see, and when it does, just make sure you make the most of it. Another coffee?"

"No thanks, I really must be getting around to that shop, there's still quite a bit of unpacking to do. I'll still be at it until the early hours at this rate."

"Why should you, Gladys, there's always tomorrow? You've got to remember that now, there's only you to please. So, there's still a box standing in the middle of the room when you get up in the morning, so what? Just let it stand there, that's of course, unless you want it out of the way."

"I suppose you're right. It's just that I've never thought that way. It will take time to get used to it I guess."

"Of course it will, but that's one commodity you'll find you'll have plenty of, time. Anyway, let's show you where these shops are. I'll just get my coat."

Helen, returning from the bedroom and doing up her coat, smiled warmly at Gladys who was standing timidly by the front door. "It's not much of a shopping area really, but they've got all the basics and they're a pretty friendly lot."

Unaware that her feelings of insecurity were gradually already disappearing, Gladys followed her neighbour happily down the hall.

CHAPTER 2

The next morning, hearing the doorbell ring, Helen turned off the gas and moved quickly to answer the front door. Her heart dropped when she was greeted by a smartly dressed man in his late fifties with silver hair and a slight smile on his tanned face.

"Hello Helen."

"What do you want?"

"I thought I'd come and see how you were getting on; see if there was anything you needed."

Helen moved to close the door.

"I need you to leave me alone, Good-bye."

The man's foot moved quickly to stop the door closing.

"Wait a minute Helen, can't we be a little more civil. It's been a long time."

Looking at the foot, Helen considered stamping on it.

"Not long enough, now please go."

Placing a hand against the door, he persisted.

"We need to talk."

"We've got nothing left to talk about."

"Well actually."

"Hello, here it comes."

"What do you mean?"

"Every time you use that word 'actually', it's a cue for me or some other poor bastard to be conned. I've seen you work remember."

"All I want you to do is sign something the lawyers forgot. When they told me it had been missed, I volunteered to bring it round. It seemed a good opportunity to see if you were OK. It's as simple as that, believe me."

"Believe me," repeated Helen, "and there's two other words that starts alarm bells ringing. Two words, I wouldn't even believe from you, if you were on your death bed."

"What are you going on about?"

"Never mind. What is it that you want me to sign? Your death warrant, I hope."

Ignoring her last remark, the man placed his shoulder against the door. "Can I come in, just for a minute, it won't take long?"

Helen looked at her husband in total distrust and thought for a moment. "All right, but make it quick."

He went into the living room and looked around. "Nice place you've got here, it must have cost a fortune to fix."

"You're joking. With the amount I managed to escape with, I've had to do it all myself."

"I didn't realise you were so handy."

"I had the same ignorance about you and your bimbos it seems."

"That's all in the past now, I haven't been able to settle since we parted."

"Settle, is that what you call your away games?"

"I've been made redundant."

"The news gets better. Now what is it you want me to sign?"

He placed a slim brief case on the table and removed a

document which he held up. "This, apparently, is holding up the divorce."

She made no move take it. "What is it?"

Helen's husband placed the document on the table, and took an expensive looking pen from his inside coat pocket and offered it to her. "It's a mere formality really,"

She put on her glasses, which as usual hung around her neck, leaned over the table and began to read the top sheet without touching it.

"Actually, the Lawyers should have cleared it up at the last meeting," he mumbled.

She cast a quick glance in his direction and began to read.

He moved the pen closer. "What's wrong… just sign where the crosses are on the back page."

Helen looked at him and reached out to take the pen then hesitated. "I think I'll finish reading it all first, you always said never ever sign anything without reading it."

He snatched the document from the table and held it inches from her face. "There's no need. As I said, it's only a formality."

Helen stepped back and looked at him suspiciously. "Is that right? Why is it I don't believe you? Now give me the document or get out."

Reluctantly he handed it to her.

"Chatsford Union Pension Plan," she read out loud, starting again at the top of the front page. "Sounds like a good title." She read the rest of the document in silence and then placed it on the table. "Well, well, this seems to be saying that as your wife I am entitled to a percentage of your pension, but if I sign where those crosses are, I would be signing it all away. Am I right? No, don't bother to answer, I can see from your face."

"Actually, under the terms of the pension, because we

are in the process of getting a divorce, you won't be entitled to anything anyway."

Helen shook her head in disbelief and laughed. "You are pathetic. If what you just said were true, why would you be asking me to sign?"

Trembling with rage, he again pushed the document close to her face. "For god sake woman sign the bloody thing."

Although frightened, Helen smiled at him, enjoying the moment. "No, now get out."

"I need the money or I lose the house."

"What a shame, but as the pension is to provide for me, it's mine not yours."

"But, without the money, I can't meet the full mortgage repayments."

Helen placed her hands on her hips and stared at him. At last her moment had come. "Tough."

His hand, still holding the document, flew out and hit her across the face sending her backwards into the nearest armchair. "Bitch, you'd love to see me in the gutter."

The ringing of the doorbell, bought his verbal abuse to an abrupt halt.

Holding her cheek, Helen rose and keeping the table between them, moved quickly to open the door. "That's where you belong so you should feel quite at home."

"You've had enough out of me over the years. All that money I spent on you."

"Only because it suited you to have me around. I was acceptable to those you were trying to impress. It was you that had to impress everyone else, with the big house, the big car. Well now let's see how impressed they are?"

Helen reached the door and placed her hand on the latch.

Holding out the document, he stepped threateningly towards her. "You're going to sign this thing if I have to break every bone in your body."

Helen quickly opened the door and saw with relief her friend and neighbour standing there.

CHAPTER 3

"Hello Gladys, good to see you. Come in and meet an excuse for a man. He also happens, for the moment to be my husband but not, I'm glad to say, for much longer."

Noticing the red patch on her cheek, Gladys glanced angrily at the man.

"Did you do that?"

"He's been trying to convince me that he's fallen on hard times and got upset because I wouldn't sign over to him what is mine. Anyway, he's just leaving."

Gladys moved closer to Helen still holding the door open.

Angrily pointing a finger at her, the man stepped forward threateningly.

"I want you to leave right now; this is between husband and wife, so keep your bloody nose out of it."

Gladys kicked off her slippers and stepped away from her friend to stand in the doorway, and in a voice Helen hardly recognised asked, "Do you want the long answer or the short one?"

Roaring with rage, both arms out stretched to push her back out through the doorway, he rushed at her. Unable to move, Helen saw for an instant the legs of her husband flying through the air, before a loud thump announced his undignified landing in the hall.

An expression of determination on her face, Gladys remained in the doorway looking down at Helen's husband.

81

"Bloody hell Gladys," exclaimed Helen. "Do that again."

Struggling to his feet he pointed angrily at Gladys. "You cow, I'll get you for that."

"I really think you should go," suggested Helen, trying hard not to laugh. "Even my friend can see you've outstayed your welcome and let's face it, you're definitely not going to get your document signed."

Helen picked up the papers from the floor, the pen and brief case from the table, and threw them into the hall.

"Don't bother signing for me. I shall be writing to my solicitor to let them know where to send the monthly cheques."

Still swearing, Helen's embarrassed husband gathered up the items and stuffed them into his coat pocket, then began to limp down the hall attempting to straighten his hair and tie. "You vindictive bitch."

"Ain't that the truth?" called Helen ushering Gladys into the room and closing the door.

The two friends, stood listening to the sounds of his retreat, until it was punctuated by the slamming of the front door.

Gladys collapsed into an armchair and sighed loudly. "I think he's gone. How's the face?"

"A little sore but I've had worse."

"He's hit you before?"

"A couple of times, when he was under stress about some deal or other."

"And you stayed with him?"

"In general, it was a good life, except towards the end."

"Well, I never thought people with money, did that sort of thing."

"Oh! Gladys, they're no different from anybody else, believe me."

"What was he trying to make you sign?"

"The rights to my share of his pension."

"It must be a fair old sum if he was getting that upset about it. Obviously not a Gas Board pension. Did you know about it before?"

"Not the details. Like you I let him take care of all that, but stupidly he let me read the policy just now. It looks like my pension will be quite substantial. That's why he wanted me to sign. Do you fancy a brandy? I think I need one after all that excitement."

"I don't know. I've never tried it."

Helen took a bottle and two glasses from the cupboard. She poured a good measure into each and passed one to Gladys.

Gladys eyed the liquid, smelt it, and held up the glass. "Nice looking glasses."

"They're called balloon glasses."

"What special like, just for brandy?"

"Just for brandy," confirmed Helen.

Helen swirled the golden liquid around a couple of times, and then raised the glass in a toast to Gladys. "To you and thanks for your help."

"No problem." Gladys raised her glass in response and took a sip.

"Don't you like it?"

Gladys raised the glass to take another sip. "I wouldn't say that."

"Where did you learn to fight like that?"

"Hubby used to teach Judo. Did it for years. Sort of hobby like. Over the years he taught me a few things just in case." Gladys smiled thoughtfully and gave a little chuckle. "Didn't get very far on a lot of occasions when we were younger though; sometimes we would get side tracked, if you know what I mean."

"You mean sex?"

Gladys giggled, a little embarrassed.

"Well I'd never have thought of martial arts as a form of foreplay," laughed Helen.

"This is good," exclaimed Gladys, draining her glass. "Is it dear?"

"Can be, it depends on whether it's a good one or not. I tend to save it for special occasions. Would you like another?"

"Ta, if that's alright."

CHAPTER 4

By the end of the first week, although the big box in the middle of the living room had gone. Gladys decided after checking the Sun 'Bingo' bought earlier that morning to go with her tea and toast breakfast she would make the living room the day's priority. Everything was going well and, with her usual BBC2 programmes as company, she felt almost happy.

She opened the cupboard doors to the left of the fireplace, wrung out her wet cloth and began to wipe the shelves and floorboards. The cloth snagged on a large splinter. She lifted both cloth and attached section of floorboard out to separate them. It was only as she went to put the cut section of floorboard back in place that she noticed that those around it had also been cut into short lengths.

Gladys leaned forward for a closer look. Something black and shining in the space left by the missing floorboard, caught her eye. Taking a torch from the drawer in the cupboard on other side of the fireplace, she returned and knelt down. Light from the torch lit up what appeared to be a package about the size of a sliced loaf, wrapped in a black bin liner and held together by brown masking tape.

The removal of another section of cut floorboard revealed two more packages. She lifted them out and arranged them in front of her, then returned to the other cupboard again for a pair of scissors. Nervously she picked up the first package to cut the masking tape and tip out its contents. Four brown paper bundles held together by Sellotape tumbled out. She picked up and removed the wrapper from one of them. It took a moment for her to realise that what she held in her hand was a neat bundle of fifty-pound notes held together by two wide elastic bands.

The bundle dropped from her hand. "Oh, my gawd."

She hardly dared to look at it. She began to fold the brown paper then suddenly noticed that someone had written on the wrapping: £30,000. Checking the unopened brown paper bundles, she found that, except for one that had £32,675 written on it, they too had £30,000 on them. She clapped both hands to her mouth and, shutting her eyes tightly, hoping that the longer she kept her eyes closed the more chance there was that the money would disappear, she repeated. "Oh, my gawd."

At last she was able to open the remaining black bin liner packages, and with the use of a biro and the back of the paid moving in receipt she calculated that she, who had never seen a £50 note, or held more than a £100 in her purse, was in possession of £362,675.

"Three hundred and sixty-two thousand, six hundred and seventy-five pounds," she read out slowly. "Three Hundred and…" she repeated twice more. "What am I going to do with it?"

Unable to take her eyes off the remaining eleven brown paper packages and the single bundle of notes, it was a few moments before she could make a decision. She carefully arranged the packages in the centre of the dining room table, then took the bowl of soapy water and cloth into the kitchen, returning with a tumbler and an unopened half bottle of brandy she had bought only the day before. Her hands shook as she poured herself a large measure, and stood sipping it while gazing out of the window at the grey winter sky.

The room was almost in darkness when she eventually drew the curtains and turned on the lights to take another look at the neatly stacked bundles. She lit the gas fire and returned to the table to lift each side of the green table cloth in turn over the pile. She gave a quick polish of the exposed brown table surfaces and walked to her flat door, took a deep breath, opened it, and strode positively across the hall to ring Helen's bell.

The strange expression on her neighbour's face, made Helen wait for Gladys to speak first.

"I was wondering if you would come into my flat... if you don't mind. I need to show you something."

Helen grabbed her keys from the small table, closed her front door and followed her friend, already back at the table looking at the pile in the middle. When Gladys didn't say anything, Helen asked. "What's the problem?"

Without a word Gladys went into the kitchen and returned with a seagull-decorated tumbler. She poured a good measure of brandy and handed it to Helen, then she topped up her own glass. "Sorry about the seagulls."

"Bit early for brandy isn't it Gladys?"

"You did say it was good for special occasions... I think you'll agree this is one of them."

Gladys placed the bottle on the mantelpiece and raised her glass to her neighbour. She took a drink, then approached the table.

Helen watched as one by one each side of the green cloth was lifted to reveal a pile of brown paper bundles. Unsure of what was expected of her, she looked at her friend. "What's this?"

"If… when you see what it is, you decide to leave, I shall understand."

"This must be serious. You robbed a bank or something?" Helen placed her glass on the corner of the table, as Gladys handed her the bundle of notes. "Good heavens, you have robbed a bank."

"No, I didn't rob a bank, but I think someone did." Gladys pointed at the brown bundles on the table and then at the cupboard. "I found all these under the floorboards in that cupboard, when I was washing it out."

"There must be thousands," suggested Helen.

"Three hundred and sixty-two thousand, six hundred and seventy-five pounds to be exact."

Helen held out her glass for a refill. "That's a bloody lot of brandy."

Gladys took the bottle from the mantelpiece and shared what was left between both glasses. "What do you think I should do with it, turn it over to the police?"

Immediately Helen replied. "Only as a last resort."
Gladys looked at her friend questioningly.

"I just think that first we should try and figure out who put it there."

"Any ideas?" asked Gladys.

Helen bent down and picked up the discoloured newspaper lying discarded on the floor. "Was this the liner covering the floorboards?"

Gladys nodded.

"February last year," read Helen. "Must have been that horrid little man that use to live here before you came." Helen looked at the ceiling as if seeking divine inspiration. "What was his name?" The room remained silent for a moment. "No, it's gone. Maybe I'll remember it later?"

Gladys sat down on one of the dining room chairs positioned around the table. "Any idea where he is now?"

"No idea, the last time I spoke to the landlord, he said that he hadn't received any rent or even heard from him for months. He talked about moving the man's stuff to the cellar and finding a new tenant. I think he also mentioned reporting him as missing to the police. Next thing I knew, a company was here packing his stuff and changing the locks. Five weeks later you arrived."

Still holding the bundle of notes, Helen took a chair opposite her friend and sat looking at them in silence for some time. "Three hundred and sixty-two thousand pounds," she said suddenly.

"Three hundred and sixty-two thousand, six hundred and seventy-five pounds," corrected Gladys.

Not looking away from the bundle, Helen mumbled. "Exactly."

Gladys picked up the empty bottle. "Another?"

Holding up the bundle close to her ear, Helen flicked the end of the notes with a smile. "Saw that done in a movie once."

Gladys wavered the empty bottle at Helen. "Brandy?"

"Most definitely." Helen drained her glass, rose and walked unsteadily to the front door. "I'll get some re-enforcements. I'll close the door, but make sure it's me when I come back."

For a moment she remained standing at the door looking back at Gladys, trying to figure out if what she had said made sense.

"What did you say?" asked Gladys.

"I'll knock three times."

A little later two knocks, followed by a pause and then a single knock, brought Gladys out of her trance. She walked unsteadily to the door and opened it.

"How many knocks was that?" asked Helen closing the door behind her.

Back sitting down at the table, Gladys replied. "Three… I think."

"Harrison, that was his name, little weasel man, Birmingham accent, sounded a bit like Beryl Reed. 'Evening each. The name's 'arrison – 'array 'arrison'," mimicked Helen in a bad brummie accent before removing the cap from an almost full bottle of brandy.

"Reinforcements."

CHAPTER 5

Helen moved her chair closer to the table and poured brandy liberally in to each glass and raised her own to toast her friend. "To your good fortune, it couldn't have happened to a nicer person."

"Hear, hear, hic, sorry. I've been thinking, if the money does belong to this Harry bloke, why hasn't he come back for it? Or, or why didn't he use it to pay his rent?"

Helen considered the question for a moment, "Maybe he couldn't?"

"Why not?"

The brandy making it difficult to concentrate, Helen hesitated. "Well the three reasons that spring to mind, assuming that he is a criminal. A fact I am almost certain of." She began to count with the aid of her fingers, "He is either in Prison, he has had a loss of memory or he's dead."

"Why?" asked Gladys.

Helen held her open hand up and began to push her fingers down one by one. "Sentenced by court, hit on the head by a Lollipot lady, murdered by people wanting their share of the money."

"Lollipot lady?" repeated Gladys with a giggle. "Did you say Lollipot?"

"Afraid I might have, it's probably the brandy."

"OK, but where did he get the money?"

"Who knows, but he was definitely a shifty looking individual, with a hook nose and going bald."

"Criminal type?" asked Gladys.

"Definitely."

Gladys nodded towards the bundles on the table. "So, what we going to do with them?"

"Initially nothing other than move them. That way if anyone comes to collect, it's gone."

"But they will think that I took it."

"Then you'll have to act dumb."

Gladys paused for a moment, before a smile began to slowly appear on her face and she began nodding her head. "I can do that, in fact, I've been doing it most of my life, only it wasn't acting. Let others make the decisions. What do I understand? Just let it happen, that's me. My mother was the same. I can still remember the struggle she had when my dad left, but did I learn, nah! So, when it was my turn, I finished up here. Do you think that's dumb enough to fool anyone?"

Helen paused, before giving Gladys a sympathetic smile. "Should suffice."

"Well now it's too late to do anything about the past, but from this moment, I'll say what goes. Which shouldn't be too difficult when you consider that there is only me?"

The friends sat in silence once again staring at the money. Finally, Gladys said, "Helen, I've been thinking. I'd like to improve myself in some ways, talk better perhaps, dress with a little more style, not sound as though I'm apologising all the time… be more like you."

Helen put down her glass and lent across the table to take hold of Gladys's hands. "Thank you for the compliment, but I wouldn't exactly consider myself a role on which to model a new you." She took a couple of deep breaths and tried hard to concentrate. "I think, no hang on, that's not right. I don't think that you should use me as a model on which to base a new you, especially when it comes to making decisions. OK, the dress thingy maybe, the 'spleech' or even speech likewise. But although I'm really flattered, when you consider some of the stupid decisions I've made, well you've met one of them,"

"But will you help me?"

"If that's what you really want, I'd be only too happy to oblige."

"Good, now about this money; I think you're right Helen, we've got to find a new hiding place."

Helen smiled. "Is that your decision?"

Looking at each other they both began to laugh.

"I think we should toast to you making a decision," suggested Helen, as their laughter subsided.

"So do I… I think?" agreed Gladys, starting to laugh again. "How about putting it temporarileee, tempora… temp… Oh! Shit, for the present in your place?"

"Suppose I'm burgled?"

Gladys took hold of the table to steady herself, even though she was sitting down. "What made you think of that?"

"Why not, it happens nearly every day around here."

Gladys thought for a moment. "How about we hide it in the same place, but in your flat?"

"Supposing my floorboards don't lift?"

"My hubby, besides being good at judo, was also a dab hand at carpentry," said Gladys.

Helen started to giggle.

Gladys, also giggling suddenly stopped. "What's funny about being good at woodwork?"

"I was wondering how one used woodwork as a form of foreplay."

"You're sex mad." Gladys laughed. "Mind you I remember one time, he was using his Black and Decker workbench." Gladys stopped suddenly.

"And," urged Helen.

"Err, no not now, some other time. Let's go and have a look at your floorboards."

"A wise decision," agreed Helen. "Brandy?"

Gladys held her glass out unsteadily. "Why not?"

CHAPTER 6

Two weeks had passed in which time the floorboards had been cut and the money transferred, as planned, to Helen's flat when Gladys opened her front door in response to a knock. She was confronted by two men, one dressed in a smart designer suit and tie, the other, a bigger built individual in leather bomber jacket and Jeans. The smartly-dressed one standing in front spoke. "Good morning madam, we're from the council."

"Oh yes,"

Gladys, only too aware from her many years as a council tenant and knowing what a council worker should look like, instinctively pushed the door slightly to reduce the gap.

"We are carrying out a survey on the facilities provided in private rented flats."

She saw his eyes attempting to look over her shoulder into her flat and she knew her suspicions were right.

"We were wondering if we could look around your flat?"

"What, both of you?"

"My colleague is learning the ropes."

"Is that so? Do you have any identity?"

"Err, well actually, we're normally working inside, so we don't usually need it."

"Well you do to get in here. Good morning,"

She shut the door before they could object. The man in the leather jacket started banging on it loudly. "'Ere, we want to talk to you."

"Come back when you've got some ID, and make sure you bring a copper."

Helen who had heard the voice in hall, opened her door and stood looking at the two men. "Can I help you?"

The man in the suit pushed his companion towards the stairs. "No, it's OK we're from the council."

"What department?"

"Sorry madam, we can't stop we're in a bit of a rush this morning."

The man in the leather jacket received another push and they both made a hasty exit down the stairs.

Helen continued to lean against her doorway until she heard the front door slam before crossing the hall and knocking on Gladys's door. "It's me. They've gone."

Gladys opened her door and looked towards the stairs.

"Were they really from the council?" asked Helen.

"No way. I've been dealing with council people all my life and that's the first time I've seen one wearing a flash designer suit."

"So, who were they?"

Gladys pointed through her open front door at the cupboard in which the money had been hidden. "By the look of them, I'd say that they had something to do with 'IT'."

"Maybe they were just burglars casing the place for later?" suggested Helen.

"Helen, where were you educated? Thieves dressed like that do not go around asking to look at these sorts of places. They can see from the outside, there's nothing worth stealing. The scruffy opportunist burglar, now he's something different: a video here,

93

a purse there, but those little toe rags would be dressed in track suits and trainers. Not designer suits and silk ties. No, I'd lay even money they were mates of your Mr Harrison."

Gladys moved back into her flat followed by her neighbour.

"So, what are we going to do about it?" asked Helen.

Gladys walked to the living room window and looked down on to the street. "Fancy a coffee?"

"I'll put the kettle on," offered Helen.

"Hang on, come here quick, it's one of those men," exclaimed Gladys.

Helen quickly joined her friend at the window and they watched the man in the leather jacket climb into a van parked across the street. After sometime had passed without them driving away Gladys turned away from the window. "Do you know what I think, Helen? I think they know the money should be in that cupboard. But knowing they can't search the flat with me here. I reckon they're going to watch this place until I go out. Then they'll be up here like a dose of salts and straight to that cupboard."

"I think you're right," agreed Helen.

"What happens when they find it's gone? They might guess that I've taken it."

"We've got to think of a way to convince them that you know nothing about it."

"And ensure that they don't come back," added Gladys.

"How about we make it look like we're going shopping, but instead, we watch them from up the road. Then if they do break in, we ring the police, which with luck should give them enough time to check out the cupboard and see that the money's gone before they arrive."

Gladys was not yet convinced about the plan. "What happens when they're released?"

"With luck, they'll know the cash is not here and keep

their distance, especially if they know the coppers are aware of their interest. As you said yourself, who but an opportunist would rob this sort of place."

"Supposing they don't break in?"

"Then, we just report two suspicious looking characters in a van."

Gladys hardly gave herself any time to think about it. She looked at her gran's clock. "It's one o'clock. What time do you think we should leave?"

"Why not now? Get your coat on and we'll meet in the hall."

As they reached the local underground station, they became aware that they had been followed by the man in the leather jacket. They were forced to buy tickets, but then watched from the other side of the barrier until he left. Following him back to the end of their street, they were just in time to see the two men cross the road and enter their building.

Gran's clock struck two as the front door to Gladys' flat opened and the two men entered. The man in the suit returned a credit card to his wallet and made his way directly to the left-hand cupboard.

"Right Charley, clear the bottom out and let's see if that little shit Harrison was lying."

Down on to his knees, Charley quickly removed the contents and floorboards. Then lying on his stomach slid forward until his head was in the cupboard.

"Well?" asked his companion impatiently.

"Nuffing, Bob, nuffing at all."

"There must be, here let me have a look."

Charley backed out and stood up. "I tell yer, there's nuffing there."

Bob crouched down so as not to dirty his suit and peered into the cupboard's dim interior.

"This must be the place; the floorboards have even been cut, like Harrington said."

Up again, standing alongside his mate, Bob looked at the items Charley had pulled out of the cupboard. Bending down, he picked up the newspaper that had been used as a liner.

"February last year; it's even the right bloody month. Check that other cupboard."

Clearing some of the contents from the other cupboard, Charley looked inside. "The floorboards ain't even cut. I reckon the old girl's moved it."

"Does she look like she's worth three hundred thousand?" responded Bob. "Look at the place; she's hardly surviving now. No, it has to be somebody who was in it with him."

"But that was us."

"I know that you pillock… somebody we don't know about."

Three loud knocks on the door stopped Bob from venting his feelings any further.

"This is the police. Open up."

"Bloody hell," whispered Bob, "someone must have spotted us coming in. Quick, shove that stuff back in the cupboard. They mustn't find out what we've come for, just in case they find Harry's body."

The door burst open, this time with the aid of a boot and two uniformed police officers entered, followed by one in civvies.

"We'll if isn't our friend's, Bob and Charley," he said, "and just what little caper are you two up too?"

"Nothing, we're just waiting for a mate," answered Bob.

"Oh yeah, and what's your mates name?"

"Tom Smith," answered Charley quickly.

Bob, gazed in disbelief at his mate and then at the

ceiling. "Oh, well done super brain, that's really original," he whispered.

"What's wrong with Smith?" protested Charley.

"Right you two, I'm arresting you on suspicion of breaking and entering. You have no need to say…"

His words were interrupted by Gladys as she entered the room with Helen close behind. "'Ere, what you lot doing in my flat?" she protested, going into her act.

"And you are?" asked the CID officer.

"Gladys Fenton. This is my flat."

I'm Sergeant Sillett CID. We had a tip off that two men sitting in a van across the road were acting Skillet suspiciously. We arrived just in time to see them enter through the front door. They've obviously targeted your flat for some reason, so I am arresting them for breaking and entering."

Gladys a concerned look on her face looked around the room. "Oh, my gawd, have they taken anything?"

"Nuffing worth taking." muttered Charley.

Bob, elbowed his mate in the ribs. "Shut up you prat. You and your big mouth. Just button it will yer."

"Now girls no fighting. Just what did you break in for? Surely banks are more in your line, Bob?"

"We came to the wrong flat, didn't we?"

"You mean you meant to rob some other flat?"

"So why have my cupboards been emptied?" asked Gladys, drawing attention to the open doors and contents lying around. "They've even cut out the floorboards in this one."

The CID officer crouched down to take a closer look into the cupboard and then looked at the short lengths of floorboard laying on the floor. "My guess is that something has been hidden in there."

He stood up and focused on Bob. "I wonder what that

could have been? Wasn't something your old mate Harry Harrison was keeping for you, was it Bob? Like the money from the Lewisham Gas Board robbery."

"That was the name of the tenant who had this flat before Gladys," exclaimed Helen, now beginning to play her role.

"Harry! We ain't seen him for years," protested Bob. "Anyway, we ain't even got a saw with us."

"I believe he would have had to cut the boards before he could hide the money under them, don't you think?" suggested the sergeant, his voice heavy with sarcasm. "In which case – and you can correct me if I'm wrong – you would not have needed a saw."

Bob and Charley stared at the cupboard without answering.

"I suppose you're also going to tell me," continued the sergeant in the same vein, "that you never knew he used to live here, either?"

"Course not, how would we know?"

The CID officer sighed heavily and turned to the two uniformed constables standing by the door.

"OK lads, take them down the station and book them."

Gladys and Helen watched in silence as the two men were handcuffed.

"Did you know Mr Harrington?" asked the sergeant addressing Helen as they were led out through the door.

"Only in passing. Mr Lombard, our Landlord, told me he'd disappeared without paying his rent and that he was going to store his things in the cellar just in case he ever did came back.

"Can I tidy up now?" asked Gladys.

"Sorry, but we'll need to get forensics to check for finger prints before you put it all back."

The officer pointed at the cupboard and floorboards.

"By the way Mrs Fenton, did you know that those boards could lift out?"

"No. I've only just moved in, so all I've done is shove those things in there, when I first arrived." Gladys pointed to the sheets of newspaper lying on the floor. "Haven't even got around to changing that liner that was in the bottom."

The officer picked it up. "February last year, even the right month."

"What was that?" asked Helen.

"Last February there was a robbery of Gas Board wages. The money has never been recovered. When Harrison wasn't seen around for a while we began to suspect that he had been involved and was lying low for a bit. Unfortunately, we could never find any proof. Now, finding those two obviously looking for something, in what was his flat, could mean that they may have been involved as well."

The officer strolled towards the front door and stopped to look back. "I'll be on my way now, the finger print people should be here in an hour. If you find anything missing make sure you let me know. Oh, by the way I'll send someone round to replace your lock. I'm afraid we had to kick it open, Good afternoon."

Helen and Gladys remained standing in the middle of the room, listening to the ticking of Gran's old clock until hearing the sound of the police car being started and driven away.

Helen looked out the window on to the street. "They've gone, so has the van."

Gladys let out a big sigh of relief and collapsed into an armchair. Sitting on the arm next to her, Helen put a comforting hand on her friend's shoulder. "I think it's an occasion."

Gladys looked up at Helen, and gave her a smile, "I'll get the brandy and we'll toast whoever made that phone call."

99

Getting up, Helen made to leave, her front door key in her hand. "I'll get the glasses. Leave those seagulls of yours in the cupboard – this occasion must be done properly."

CHAPTER 7

Gladys turned on the living room light and glanced at her grans clock before returning to sit in the armchair opposite Helen. "Four forty and it's getting dark already. Do you know it's nearly four weeks since those two blokes broke in here? Do you think we'll hear any more about them?"

Helen drank the last of her coffee. "It doesn't look like it, but then the police don't always move that fast. What made you ask?"

"I was thinking."

"What, about the money?"

"What else?"

"Anything in particular?"

"Spending some of it."

Helen placed her empty mug on the floor alongside her armchair. "On what?"

"How about a holiday?"

"That sounds nice, anywhere particular?"

"Anywhere you like, maybe abroad, but you choose. After all, now we've agreed to share, you've as much right to pick a place as I have and anyway, I'm sure you know better places then I do. I've never even had a passport."

"Good lord, why's that?"

"Simple, we could never afford a reason to get one."

Helen thought for a while. "Well the first thing we'd have to do is change some of the money, just in case the police have a list of the numbers."

"What do you mean, we can't just go out and spend it?"

"Too risky, if they do have the numbers of the notes, they could trace them back to us. So, we have to change the notes a bit at a time. They call it laundering, I think."

"How about, we just ask them if they know the numbers?" asked Gladys, "That way we wouldn't have to, err… launder."

"You can't do that Gladys; they'd want to know why we're interested."

"So, we hand two fifty-pound notes to that CID bloke and say we found them hidden in the kitchen cupboard or somewhere. If he keeps them because they are part of the robbery, he's bound to tell us they know the numbers and if he hands them back, we know they don't know the numbers. Gladys held up her hand to stop Helen from replying. "Hang on a minute though. It would be better if we used two real notes. That way they can never say that some of the stolen money was actually found in the flat. I'm sure he'd still tell us if they knew the numbers."

Helen laughed, impressed by her friend's plan. "That sounds rather sneaky, are you sure you haven't done this sort of thing before?"

Gladys rang the bell to Helen's flat.

"You're back already," Helen exclaimed, pulling her inside. "How'd you get on?"

"That CID bloke seems pretty sure that they don't have the numbers, but is going to check anyway."

Gladys followed Helen into her kitchen and watched as she filled the kettle. "He says that the two men who broke into my flat are currently out on bail. Oh! and that Harrison bloke still hasn't been found. They suspect that those two men may have something to do with his disappearance."

"Did he mention how long it would take to check on the numbers?"

"About two weeks, he'll let me know as soon as he hears."

The estimate turned out to be correct, for on answering a knock on her front flat door two weeks later. Gladys was confronted by the CID officer holding up her two fifty-pound notes.

"Hello Sergeant. Come in I'll put the kettle on."

"It's OK Mrs Fenton. I'm on another call. I'm only here to return your money and let you know there is no record of the numbers stolen."

A broad grin spread across her face as she accepted the two notes and folded them before slipping them into her apron pocket.

"So, do you think it will be alright if I put them towards a holiday? Or should I keep them in case Mr Harrington does come back?"

"That's looking less and less likely. We've now run out of sources which might have been able to help us with our enquires. So, unless we find his body the whole thing is going to go nowhere. If I were you, I'd spend the money and enjoy it. But you never heard that from me."

Gladys excited at the news and hearing the front door downstairs close, grabbed her keys and hurried across the hall.

"Well I guess that means we can start changing the money. But to be sure, we'll not change it around here. We'll go up the West End, do a little shopping, may be even go to a theatre. The change we get, we'll put aside for the holiday."

Another few weeks had passed and the friends were sitting in the lounge talking over coffee about their plans and the news that Helen's final settlement for her divorce had come through, when a knock interrupted them.

Gladys got up and approached the door asking, "Who can this be?"

"Hello Mum."

Gladys's lips tightened as she recognised the unshaven face, grubby jeans and scuffed leather jacket of her son. "What are you doing here?"

"I've come to see you."

"Pity. I thought I'd covered my tracks better than that. On the scrounge, are we?"

Uninvited he entered the room and stood in the middle looking around him. "Now don't be like that mum."

"Why not, the only time I see you is when you want something."

Gladys remained holding the door open, hoping he would take the hint and leave. When he didn't and she realised it was just wishful thinking, she closed it and stood arms folded watching him. "This Helen, is the object I gave birth too, his name's Kevin."

Helen rose from her chair to greet him. "Hello Kevin."

Ignoring her outstretched hand, the scruffy figure continued his tour of the room, taking in its contents from furniture to familiar statues on the mantel piece.

"Don't take any notice of him Helen. He's too stupid to be rude," offered Gladys, in the way of an apology.

"It's alright I'll see you later, give us a call when you're free." Helen stopped as she reached her friend standing by the front door. "Will you be all right? I'll stay if you wish." she whispered.

"Thanks Helen, but I have no fear of this little creep."

Without speaking, Helen patted Gladys on the shoulder and left.

"So how did you find me?"

"Spoke to the Wilson woman, next door. She said you hadn't given her your new address in case I turned up."

"That's true. She's a nice woman but never could keep a secret. So how did you manage to find me?"

"The estate agent's board was still lying in the garden. I asked them."

"That was a mistake."

"Anyone would think that you were not glad to see me?"

"What gave you that impression?" replied Gladys sarcastically.

"But I'm your son."

Gladys strode towards him. "Son! What do you know about being a son? You've been nothing but trouble since you could walk." Gladys stood in front of him to poke him in the chest, and emphasis her words. "Selfish... idle... The last maternal instinct I had for you disappeared when I found out that your dad had remortgaged our home in order to pay off your debts to save you from a beating. The poor man kept it a secret from me so that I wouldn't worry about you or the roof over our heads. Do you realise the stress that put him under, forcing him to split his loyalties in that way... no I bet you don't... and if you did, I bet you bloody well wouldn't care!" She turned away and walked across the room so he wouldn't see her trying to control the urge to cry. Too much had built up in her over the years, and she needed him to know exactly the utter disgust she felt for him. Determined that for him, it would be a wasted visit Gladys took a deep breath and glared at him on the other side of the room. "You couldn't even be bothered to come to your own father's funeral."

Kevin looked away towards the clock on the cupboard. "I did come to the funeral."

"Come to the funeral?" repeated Gladys in disbelief. "You never came to the funeral. You made an appearance, which lasted less than half an hour. Then you crawled back under your stone. You never even bothered to ask how I was coping. I lost my home through your stupid selfish attitude, a home that had taken your father and me years to put together."

"I didn't know and anyway I've been busy."

Gladys remained for a moment looking at her son. No tears, no anger, just sadness. "Yeah, I bet you've been busy, earning enough to pay back what you owe me perhaps?"

Kevin's eyes moved to look down at the floor.

"No, I know that will never happen. Conning or sponging off some other poor soul is more your style."

Her hands clenched; Gladys looked unseeingly out of the window. Everything in the room had seemed to slow down, even the ticking of her gran's clock seemed to have slowed. With no more doubts, no more apologises, she realised she was at last free. It was just her. Gladys lifted her head and straightened her shoulders as the load she had been carrying disappeared. Her fists now unclenched, she turned to see that Kevin had started to circle the room again, like a shark looking for the juiciest bit. "Pricing the bits and pieces, are we?"

Kevin stopped for a moment to glance at her and looked away. "Aren't you going to offer me a cup of tea?"

Gladys shook her head in disbelief as she made her way to the kitchen leaving Kevin to focus on his mother's handbag lying on the table.

On her return she stopped in the doorway sensing the tension, her eyes instinctively drawn to her handbag.

Her son. standing by the window. turned and smiled at her and she knew. "You look different."

"In what way?"

"More..." Kevin hesitated trying to find the word, "More, modern, more with it."

Gladys strolled to the table, picked up her handbag and opened it to take out her purse.

105

"Careful, that was nearly a compliment. Have you got any money?"

"Only a couple of quid."

"I can only let you have ten pounds."

Gladys opened her purse and looked into the empty pocket, where a ten-pound note had been. "Sorry, I've only got a twenty." She closed it and returned it to her bag. She waited without looking at her son, who was making a big act of searching his pockets.

"On second thoughts, I may have a tenner somewhere." Eventually producing the stolen note from his pocket, he held it out, hardly able to stop himself from smiling at his good fortune. Gladys accepted the note and immediately put it in her purse and returned it to her handbag. Laying the bag on the table, she stood looking at him. "Thank you,"

A questioning frown of disbelief slowly appeared on his face, as he realised, he'd been tricked. "What about the twenty?"

"Don't bother saying a word Kevin, you'll only make yourself look a bigger creep than you are already. Now get out and don't even bother thinking about coming back you thieving little toe rag."

"But I owe people money. I was hoping that you would help" he whined.

"You have had all the help you are going to get, and I hope whoever it is, catches you and gives you the hammering of your life. Now get out."

"Call yourself a mother," cried Kevin.

Gladys walked quickly to the door and opened it. "You obviously have not been listening, so I'll try putting it to you one last time." Gladys moved to stand in front of him, and again began prodding his chest with her finger, pushing him backwards towards the open door.

"I am Gladys Fenton; I am a forty-five-years-old and a widow. You managed to bring that about, almost entirely on your own and now you must be feeling very proud of yourself. At present I am happier than I have been since your father died. Now this situation may change, it may not. But I'm bloody determined that I'm going to live the rest of my life my way. So, I don't want you popping back into it anytime you find yourself in need of a hand out. In other words, you do not exist." Gladys paused for a breath and watched his shocked unshaven face as the message slowly sank in, before giving him a final shove out into the hall with the flat of her hands. "Now get out and grow up you useless prat."

Slamming the door in his face, Gladys moved to stand behind the nearest armchair. She held on to the back of it with both hands as tears began to darken the faded pattern.

CHAPTER 8

Gladys looked again at the little wine-coloured book and waved it at Helen, still unable to believe that she actually had a passport. "…and in only four hours I'll be using it for the first time."

Helen, sitting opposite her in the other armchair, smiled at seeing her friend's excitement. "Have you finished your packing?"

"Two days ago, only got to put on my new glad rags, tidy my hair and I'll be ready. Can hardly wait. I've got such a lot of catching up to do."

"I know pet, I know… and it makes me happy to see you so excited."

"It's funny, but I can't even imagine what it's going to be like."

"Think of a holiday in England with a lot more sun and

a lot warmer, where most of the places actually want to serve you but ask what you want with an accent."

Helen watched the smile on her friend's face glowing with excitement. She stood up and moved towards the flat door. "How about we get ourselves ready and go to the airport early, then we can have a cup of coffee and relax?"

Only too happy to be on her way, Gladys instantly agreed. "Great idea."

Helen opened the door and stepped out into the hall. "I'll see you in a bit."

Some twenty minutes later she returned and put her case and shoulder bag down by the front door. "I'm back Gladys," called Helen as she sat down in an armchair to wait for her friend to appear. When she did, she hardly recognised the smart sophisticated lady coming from the bedroom. "Wow, Gladys, you look like a million dollars. Where have you been hiding yourself all this time?"

Still not convinced that she could carry off her new look, Gladys inspected herself in the mirror. "Do I really look alright?"

"Alright! You look bloody marvellous."

"I can't seem to get the hair right."

"Sit down. It won't take a jiff."

"Do you think we'll get away with it?"

"You mean the money... of course we will. Why are you having second thoughts?"

Gladys turned to look up at her friend. "Well, I'd be lying if I said I didn't, but then, I think of how hard my Alf worked all those years. Out in all weathers, sometimes up to his knees in dirty smelly water... and then how they treated him at the end. He always used to say, 'Gladys girl you go out and have a good time, I'll be alright. We'll enjoy time together when I retire.' Well, in the end he wasn't alright, was he?"

Helen continued doing Gladys's hair without speaking.

108

"But that crook of a chairman and all his cronies were, weren't they? Awarding themselves all that money, they never even got their hands dirty. It's when I think of things like that, the guilty feeling disappears and it makes me more determined to have a good time. I just hope Alf can see me, because I know he would understand and approve. I only wish it could have been the chairman's own money that had been stolen."

Helen patted her friend on the shoulder. "You'll do, have a look in the mirror."

Gladys stood to study herself in the mirror and smiled with approval. "You know Helen, I've realised since he's been gone, that perhaps Alf's hands weren't so dirty. At least he could wash it off when he came home. Which is more than his governors with all their 'hand outs and shares' can do."

Two sharp taps on the door stopped any further discourse on the subject.

Helen opened it and stood aside to let a smart distinguished looking man to enter. "Mr Lombard, come in."

Gladys, dabbing the corner of each eye to remove the signs of emotion, turned to face him.

"You two look dolled up. Off somewhere nice?"

"We're about to go off on two weeks holiday in Spain."

"Well I hope you have a nice time. With two lovely tenants like you staying here I'll have to put the rent up."

Helen gave Gladys a wink.

"Cup of coffee or tea Mr Lombard?"

"No thank you Mrs Fenton. Only popped in for a moment. Mrs Lombard is waiting in the car, so I mustn't be too long."

"I just wanted to make sure that you were both OK, after the break-in."

"Fine thanks, we're well over it now," replied Helen.

"Why didn't you let me know Mrs Fenton?"

"There was nothing you could have done, and the police did replace the lock."

"It was only when they called round the other evening that I found out about your break in. Otherwise I'd have been here sooner. Apparently, they've found Mr Harrison's body and are going to charge the two men that broke in here with his murder."

"What did the police want with you?" asked Gladys.

"They wanted to collect his stuff from the cellar."

"Do you think we should tell them that we're going on holiday, just in case they want to search the flat for the money?" asked Gladys.

"No, I don't think it will be necessary. They were saying that it's all probably gone by now, anyway. Well I hope you both have a good time."

"Thank you." responded Helen.

The landlord walked to the open doorway and looked back. "Good bye, see you on your return."

Helen watched him disappear down the stairs before closing the flat door.

"What do you reckon?" asked Gladys.

"You heard what the police said. They think the money's gone already."

Both stood for a moment with their own thoughts.

"Do you realise?" said Helen suddenly. "By this evening we shall be sipping those sexy cocktails."

Gladys glanced at the clock. "Look at the time. We'd better get a move on."

"I'll call a taxi," volunteered Helen.

Twenty minutes later, the sound of the two friends singing their own rendition of *We're off to Sunny Spain* could be heard as they descended the stairs to the waiting Taxi.

THE INVITATION

Nancy stepped up close to the younger of the two security men on the gate so he would catch a hint of her perfume and gave him one of her professional smiles as she held up the invitation.

"N Gain."

Unable to stop himself from taking a serious second look at her low-cut summer frock he read the name on the invitation and ticked it off on his list.

"By the way young man, where's the bar?"

"It's that green and white stripped tent across the lawn in front of the big house miss."

Her entrance achieved, Nancy leaned forward on her stiletto heels to prevent them from sinking and stepped on to the lawn. Deliberately smiling back at any man brave enough or lecherous enough to acknowledge her, she entered the tent.

She stood behind a tall man with greying sideburns, already at the crowded bar. She peered around him to see how many more were waiting to be served.

"We could be in for a long wait; the barman is all on his own would you believe. I've been trying to catch his eye for some time but he hasn't even looked this way once."

Nancy looked up into a strong handsome face and a pair of very blue eyes. "And there's me as dry as the Sahara," she said using her smile again.

"If you tell me what you'd like, when he does eventually look this way, I'll order for both of us,"

"What have they got?"

"Alcohol wise, only red or white wine I'm afraid but it is free."

"Is that all?" *Perhaps using the invitation had not been such a good idea after all*, she thought.

"Afraid so, unless you want something sparkling?"

"That sounds more interesting, I'm rather fond of bubbly."

A grin spread across his face. "Its only water I'm afraid."

"Smart arse," she snapped, at the same time cursing the person who had written the invitation. *They should be sued under the Trade Descriptions Act. A selection of free drinks will be available indeed.*

The man waved unsuccessfully at the fraught barman. "Sorry, perhaps it wasn't such a good joke."

Nancy stepped into the space next to him, vacated by a departing customer. It was then that she noticed his brilliant white dog collar. "Oops, sorry about the smart arse."

Without taking his eyes off the barman, his hand reached up to touch it. "No problem. At least it was straight talking. More than you can say for most of this lot with their politics and back stabbing and they're not exactly a fun lot."

The man's arm rose again suddenly to wave at the confused young barman as he glanced towards them in an attempt to decide who was next. "Two large red wines please. There's a couple of urgent cases here."

Nancy backed away from the crowd at the bar to wait. Seeing him from the front for the first time as he approached, Nancy congratulated herself. He was one hunky good-looking bloke, dog collar or not. Not young, his greying hair was definitely distinguishing if not a little premature."

"Sorry I had to get you red. We might have lost him."

Nancy accepted the glass and took a sip. "It's not too bad. Thank you, thank you very much."

"You're welcome. Shall we go outside? It might be a little quieter."

"It's a bit like Ladies' day at Epsom," observed Nancy, seeing the other guests in their summer frocks and hats.

The man took a sip and nodded in agreement. "Yeah, the frocks do definitely brighten the place up, not like the blokes in their blacks and blues. Take the women away and we could be at a funeral."

Nancy continued to eye her companion approvingly as she sipped her wine. He was most likely bright and cheery, definitely not a stick in mud spouting fire and brimstone. And with those shoulders he definitely looked fit.

"By the way, the name's Norman. I'm from the Eco church at the end of South Street in town."

"I'm Nancy. Pleased to meet you."

"So, what's your involvement with the archbishop?"

Nancy choked a little as the wine went down the wrong way. "Did you say Archbishop?"

"Yes, he's the top gun that organises this shindig every year. I thought you might be on one of his committees?"

Her thoughts went to the invitation and she mentally kicked herself for being so stupid. But then, how was she supposed to know it was a church do and not a Royal occasion? All the invitation had said was 'His Lordship's Garden Party'. She had looked on her attending as a business opportunity, maybe even a way of renewing acquaintance with some of her past customers.

"Are you with some charity or other?"

Knowing from experience that in her line of work it was always best to be a little truthful about one's self from the outset, she thought quickly. "Oh, nothing as grand as a committee. I only help out in a small way."

"So, what exactly do you do that got you an invitation?"

Nancy thought for a moment, wanting to word her reply carefully, "I... I help people with their stresses and hang-ups."

She could tell by the way he hesitated that he was trying to make some sense of her reply. "That sounds interesting," he began, sounding as if he really meant it. "I imagine that you would mainly deal with men?"

"Well they do seem to have more problems than the women."

"Do you have an office in town? Maybe I could come and see you sometime? Perhaps we could compare notes."

Nancy decided it was time for a bit more of the truth. "Only a small one. Most of my work involves getting out and meeting the punters – I mean people.

"Anywhere particular?"

"Mainly hotels, sometimes clubs. It's so much more sociable and comfortable than the streets as well as a lot warmer in winter. I find you also generally meet a much better class of person, plus meeting in the right surroundings I find is more persuasive."

"I can see how to meet you in the right surrounding would be far more persuasive. Our church is the same. We go out a lot to meet people in their own environment, meet them as they really are. Though, our main aim is to get them to come to our church, which I suppose is our office really. In fact, that's how I nearly didn't get in here today.

"Why, what happened?"

"I was out on the prowl for converts a couple of days ago when I lost my invitation to this shindig. Luckily the older bloke on security at the gate here is one of our flock and he just waved me through."

A thought suddenly sprung into her head. "Did you say your name was Norman?"

"That's right."

"Aren't you a Reverend or Father or something?"

"Sorry wrong church. I'm just a straight forward Mister Norman Gain."

Nancy took a big gulp of her wine and said the first thing that came into her head. "So, you can marry?"

"Good Lord yes, thank goodness. I may work for the Lord but there's got to be some fun and romance in life."

"So, where's your wife?"

"Still out there somewhere, waiting for me to ask her, I hope."

"How come?"

Looking down at her he grinned. "It's not easy to find the woman that will put up with a Bible-basher."

Obviously more than a little interested in her, Nancy took another sip of her wine and shyly looked away whispering coyly, "Why is that? Are church men so different from normal men?"

"Maybe in the more establishment churches, but I wouldn't say our lot were. Do you fancy a stroll round the estate now we're here?"

Nancy took the arm Norman had offered her and gave him one of her non-professional smiles. She dropped the invitation into the first bin they passed.

ROLLING PIN JUSTICE

I dropped the rolling pin into the sink, turned on the tap and leaned back against the worktop watching the hot water wash away the blood until my breathing and heart were almost back to normal. Turning the water off and easing the kitchen door open, I looked back up the hall.

Was he dead? He hadn't moved but I wasn't about to go any closer and check until I had to. I had time to spare and it wasn't as if he was going to go anywhere.

My brain was telling me *Think woman, think.* Then suddenly my younger years, as a production planner kicked in. *Situation! Problem! Solution.*

The Situation! One hopefully dead husband currently cluttering up the hall along with one kicked in front door.

The Problem. What to do about it?

It had been a classic seaside card from my sister, still stuck up there on the fridge door, that had started me thinking about what to do about him. It showed a big-busted woman, holding a rolling pin, waiting by the front door for her drunken husband to return. Somehow the idea had appealed to me and if I could get away with it, I'd still have a home. Whereas my original plan to walk out and disappear would have made me homeless.

I knew the chances of anyone witnessing his return were very slim. My bungalow is in a very quiet lane just outside the village, and although people at the pub might have been able to say when he left, it wouldn't have been the first time he'd sat down on the village green bench and dropped off to sleep. Plus, the neighbours either side aren't that close and are so old, they're quite deaf.

Along with the volume of their TV, they wouldn't have heard a thing and their eye-sight isn't that clever either. So I felt pretty sure they would never be called as witnesses.

So, yes definitely, I'd scrubbed my plan to just walk out and already had a new plan. I'd even chosen the weapon. It was the sound of the front door being kicked in early however that finally decided when.

Hearing it, I'd suddenly become calm and very determined, even swung the kitchen door open to see if he would fall over as he stepped into the hall. Unfortunately, he'd somehow managed to stay on his feet and had stood there in the doorway swaying and trying to focus. Then he'd seen me. "Come here bitch, I need a hand."

"Do you dear? Just coming."

I'd taken mum's old heavy wooden rolling pin from the draw and was holding it behind my back as I calmly strolled towards him.

"Hurry up, you useless cow."

"Yes dear."

My first blow had hit him on the head, straight between the eyes. I'm sure a smile must have appeared on my face as I watched him standing there for a moment trying to figure out what had happened. It was then he made a grab for the coat rack beside the front door for support, at the same time raising the other hand in a fist.

Realizing there wouldn't be enough time to select where my second blow should land, I'd just swung. Convinced I had broken at least one of his fingers holding on to the coatrack, my next target was more focused; it was his head again. After that I just continued to swing up and down, up and down making contact every time. Even as his knees bent and he sank to the floor, I didn't stop. In those short satisfying moments, he got the full twenty years of fear and beatings that I had been forced to suffer. Only when too exhausted to continue did I stop and return to the kitchen.

I gave the rolling pin a last wash with Fairy Liquid, I

rinsed it and wiped it with the tea towel then returned it to its normal place in the drawer. I rinsed the towel and hung it in its usual place on the oven door. It was now time to decide what to do about the body. With the kitchen door pushed open I studied it for a moment before warily approaching for a closer look at my problem.

I needed an alibi. Not an elaborate one, one that was feasible. One that showed I had been doing what I nearly always did at that time in the evening when my husband, poor Mr. Satchwell, was so brutally beaten to death.

Taking a deep breath, I knelt down and felt his cheek. He was beginning to feel cold but already I had the beginning of a solution. I would leave the key he'd been incapable of opening the front door with, and his rotten old cap, where they lay. I would then report finding his body and the kicked in door on my return from the shop. I might even embellish the story by saying, how I heard someone running away to explain why nothing had been stolen. My plan, I hoped, would indicate he'd been attacked after finding the front door kicked open. After all house owners don't usually kick in their own front door, especially when they have a key in their hand.

It also wouldn't be the first time I'd been forced to go out in the evening for shopping, just to feed his stupid drunken face. I took down my coat and handbag from the hallstand and returned calmly to the kitchen. I turned the light off, stepped out into the backyard, and quietly left through the back gate into the alley that runs along the back of the bungalows on this side of the lane.

Staying in the shadows I made my way to where the path comes out onto the high street, and crossed the road to our small local supermarket which is always open late.

"Hello Mrs. Satchwell, late night shopping as usual?"

Immediately I realized that I had forgotten about my

neighbour across the lane from me. Basket in hand I worded my reply carefully. "Hello Mrs Cook, yes just a few pieces for when he eventually does get home"

"Is Mr. Satchwell not home yet then?"

It would seem my alibi was still good. Nosey neighbours do have their uses.

"When was the last time you saw him come home this early?" I joked. "It's not even near closing time yet."

"Tell me about it. I swear I'll swing for my old sod one day, coming home drunk nearly every night as he does. Good night."

I watched the poor old dear shuffle her way out of the store with her late-night shopping. It was such a feeling of relief knowing that now it would never be me shuffling my way home like her. It was then I realised, I didn't really mind if I did do time. I would still have the rest of my life free of fear and in peace when I came out.

There was also the chance that Mrs. Cook might do her bit, by saying as how she had seen me before he was home. And of course, if Mum's old wooden rolling pin dried off, before the police arrived... With luck, I might not even have to do the time. Oh! but I must remember to take the postcard down off the fridge. I don't want the police getting any ideas.

A QUESTION OF CONTROL

Maisie stepped inside her apartment, shut the front door and leaned back against it; her eyes closed. For once her date had been worth the effort: good-looking, pleasant and could talk socially without being a bore. Definitely not like some of the Neanderthals the dating agency had matched her with in the past. She knew the evening had started well when she saw the pleasantly surprised look on his face as they met.

From the moment they sat down at their table however, until he had politely seen her to her taxi, not unexpectedly it had gone downhill. Even before the main course was on the table, she knew there would be no offers to exchange phone numbers or 'we must do this again sometime'. The instant the taxi door had shut he had been off without a backward glance.

She knew why it had turned out that way. After all she should, it had happened so many times in the past. She had realised a long time ago that what she did so efficiently at work as a manager did not cut ice with the men she socialized with. She would freely have admitted, if asked, that there were times when biting off her own tongue had been a real option. She would also have admitted, but only to herself, it was the reason why at forty-two she was still single and living alone.

Tonight, the eve of Valentine's Day, she had hoped she would get it right, but it wasn't to be. Even her best friend had told her once, over a second bottle of wine, "Maisie you've got the right equipment in all the right places. You're kind, gentle and a lovely person who would make some fellow a great wife. Unfortunately, you're like that scorpion, who because he couldn't swim, persuaded a frog to give him a lift across a river. Half way across he stings the frog who, as he is dying and the scorpion is drowning asks, why? To which the scorpion replies, 'I suppose because it's in my nature.' Maisie you're quite simply a control freak, which over the years you must admit, has cost you dearly."

Maisie kicked off her shoes, hung her coat and bag on the banister and entered the lounge. Twenty minutes later, a second glass of wine in her hand, stockinged-feet up on the coffee table, she reached a familiar conclusion about the evening. She was going to have to accept that there was a strong possibility there never would be a permanent relationship in her life.

Not one to dwell on self-criticism, however, Maisie took a good drink of her wine and laid her head back, allowing the late-night music to drift over her.

The next morning she rose at her usual time. After a sad recollection that it was Valentine's Day and she had no expectations, she prepared herself for yet another day at work. She liked her job and it did provide her with a comfortable life-style, so who needed men anyway? A little later, running to time, Maisie entered her local newsagents.

It was empty as usual at that time of the morning. She approached the smiling good-looking owner standing behind the counter. About her age, he had the ability to do something she did not want to lose. He was her little bit of secret sunshine; his smile was her toe-curling start for the day. Which is why, over the two years she had been getting her newspaper from his shop, she had told herself she was not interested.

True, she had been interested enough to listen in on other female customers discussing the fact that he was a widower and that those blue eyes could melt one's lip-gloss. She had not even allowed his voice and the way he talked, which she guessed was as soft as the gentle Irish mist of his homeland, to change her resolve. It was a fact, as she well knew, that if he reacted to any advances she might be silly enough to make, it would be her cue to go charging in with a desire to expedite the situation. That she knew would be the end of their uncomplicated weekday, morning only, customer client relationship.

"Good morning Miss Ainsworth how are you, this morning?"

It bothered her that she didn't know how he had found out she was a Miss, but to ask… well she knew only too well how that could end. The greeting in itself was no surprise, for he said it or something similar every weekday morning. Except this morning it somehow sounded different. This morning it was as if he was talking to her, not to one of his regular customers, as if they shared a secret.

"And 'Good morning' to you Mr…" she hesitated; there, already there was a difference, she was having to ask his name. "I'm sorry I don't know your name… and after all this time," she added a little embarrassed.

"Steve, Steve O'Conner, and is it the usual you'll be wanting?"

She could see that he wanted her to note that he had already placed her usual weekday paper on the counter. Unable to think of the simplest response, she smiled and held out her money.

He counted out her change from the till and offered it across the counter. "Would you be going to the cinema as usual this evening?"

Maisie, feeling her cheeks getting warm, cleared her throat quietly and accepted the coins. She needed to understand what was going on. "Yes… Yes, I suppose I will, but how did you know I went to the cinema?"

"Sure. Haven't I stood behind you these many weeks as we've queued to get in?"

She felt the little control she may have regained slip away. It was the way he had said, "We've queued to get in."

Maisie nodded and smiled as he continued to talk, without her understanding a word. Recovering a little, she stammered another apology. "Sorry, miles away, what was it you were saying?"

"I was saying it's an action film tonight, although I do believe it has some romance in it."

"Good... Good." Confused she turned to leave.

"Don't forget your paper, and maybe I'll see you in the queue?"

Masie turned back and accepted the paper he was holding out.

"If you like, I'll save you a place Mr. O'Conner."

Her mouth froze, she had just done the very thing she had vowed not to do; she had tried to take control. She was convinced that what they had was all over. She gave him a last sad look, only to receive one of his toe-curling smiles.

"That would be very nice of you, and the name's Steve."

"Steve," she repeated huskily as she headed for the door. Her hand on the door handle, desperately trying to think of something to say Maisie pressed her lips together to check her lipstick and looked back, "Maisie, Maisie Ainsworth."

"Maisie," he repeated, with a smile that again had her checking her lipstick.

Outside she closed the door behind her and she stood to fold the paper so it would fit in to her shoulder bag. She'd actually got a date. A pink envelope fell from between the pages of the paper. She bent down and picked it up, then looked up and down the street before opening it. She couldn't quite understand the neatly written words on the inside of the Valentine card, so she read them again and then a third time to convince herself it really did say: *'See you in the queue'*.

Convinced that she was no longer in control, she tossed her hair back and began to walk quickly towards the station. The tapping of her high heels echoed happily off the terraced houses either side of the narrow street.

THE WEIGHT ESCAPE

"Step up two, three, down two, three, keep it going, Mr Burton."

Encouraged by the pretty young trainer, Jim dug deep, ignoring his tiredness. He didn't care too much that he was the only male amongst all the females with their shorts, leotards and bouncing bits and pieces. He was carrying enough of them himself.

He'd struggled to get on buses and had got stuck in cinema seats, and experienced all sorts of similar predicaments, for such a long time now that he hardly got embarrassed anymore. The thing was he knew he wasn't meant to be like that. Up to the age of twenty he too had been in a similar condition to the young woman taking the class.

Then Mum had died. Two months later, his long-time girlfriend had dumped him and with it had gone his joy for football, squash, even life. Now he had become the grotesquely overweight shape that couldn't work, and normally only ventured out after dark.

Sure, he would never be a smooth-talking charmer like his brother, but then he didn't want the hassle of divorces and child payments that came with it. He could be happy with just the occasional smile or casual chat with a pretty girl on the bus or train. As it was, he couldn't even share the same seat.

Well last Christmas and New Year with its loneliness had been the crunch time. He was going to change his shape or die in the attempt. He'd even given his plan a name: 'The Weight Escape'. Whether it would solve all his problems, he didn't know, but as he kept telling himself. Step one, just might lead to step two.

Already after only eight exhausting weeks, with the

new diet, walking the streets every night and the five weeks of step aerobics he could feel he was making progress. Whether anybody else could see it was doubtful, as outwardly there were as yet not many signs of a slimmer Jim emerging.

The music suddenly stopped. So suddenly in fact he carried on for another step up before realising. Seeing the delectable Sally approaching while applauding her class and thanking them for putting in the effort, he remained where he was to catch his breath.

"Thank you ladies and gentleman, you're all doing really well. See you on Thursday and Mr Burton I think you're definitely getting the hang of it."

Jim gave her a big smile of appreciation. "Thank you miss, I mean Sally."

Jim walked to the edge of the hall, stacked his step on top of the others and grabbed his towel. Face and neck dry of sweat and just having put on his track suit bottoms, he was surprised as two women called out, "Good night Jim," as they left the hall.

Only having time to call back, "Night," he watched them disappear through the door before putting on the top.

It had been a long time since any woman had spoken to him first. He left the gym, his confidence higher than he could remember for a very long time, and began the walk home. The evening air cooled his hot face as he turned into Stanley Street and prepared to quicken his pace.

"Evening."

Jim stopped to look around unsure where the woman's voice had come from. As he began walking again, he spotted her standing in the shadows by an open front door, about to deposit a full bag into a large bin.

"Evening" he replied as he drew level with her front gate.

"Been to the leisure centre?" she asked.

"Yeah, step aerobics, trying to lose weight."

"Are you winning?"

"Tonight I felt for the first time that I'm actually making a little headway, but there's nothing to show for it yet."

The young woman stepped out from behind the bin into the light from her open front door. "I wish I could get that feeling."

He immediately saw that like him, she too, had a weight problem. Even from where he was standing, he could see the sadness in her pretty face. "Do you exercise?"

"No, too embarrassed to go out."

"I know the feeling; I only go walking in the evenings when it's dark?"

"I've thought about it, but, it's a bit too dangerous for a woman on her own around here after dark."

"Have you no one that you could go with?"

The woman looked down at herself. "This also brings loneliness."

"I know exactly what you mean," agreed Jim sympathetically. "You could always join me if you wanted." The words came out so quickly it surprised him. "I walk most evenings, it's part of my 'Weight Escape' plan."

A hint of a smile appeared on her face, "Your what plan?"

"Weight Escape! It's like 'Great Escape', only instead of removing the dirt from the tunnel by which to escape a prison camp, the plan is to remove the weight and escape the imprisonment of being on my own."

Smiling, the woman moved towards her front door. "It sounds a great idea but I just don't like people looking at me."

Jim looked up and down the street at the houses with

their drawn curtains. "How many people can you see at this moment, looking at me?"

The woman glanced quickly up and down the road and shook her head. "None."

"Exactly they're all too busy watching television."

"I'd hold you back."

"Only for the first couple of weeks," he coaxed. "Then I'd probably be panting after you."

The woman laughed as the expression on Jim's face changed when he realised what he had implied. "Sorry, I didn't mean it quite like that."

"It would have been nice if you had, but there'll be no one panting after me while I look like this."

"Then all the more reason for doing some panting of your own and come walking with me tomorrow night."

Jim watched her raise her head to look at him. He knew she had decided.

"Right, I will."

"I'll call for you at seven and together we'll find the real people inside ourselves."

For a moment as she stepped through the front door, he saw the sadness in her face lift. "I'll see you at seven o'clock then, and thank you."

Jim, his confidence now having risen even higher, stepped out along the street thinking to himself. Could this mean he was about to take that step two already?

ABOUT THE AUTHOR

Born in 1939, Derek retired from the Petrochemical Industry as an Engineer in 2004. He enjoys writing and trying to make what he writes a good read. Having had some competition success at Writing Club level, he decided to try and get published. To date his success is published in two Anthologies:

"Natural Recycle" in
Snowflakes
Published by Bridge House (2015)

>Order from Amazon:

>Paperback: ISBN 978-1-907335-40-2
eBook: ISBN 978-1-907335-41-9

"Bottled Christmas Spirit" in
The Best of CaféLit 7
Published by Chapeltown Books (2018)

>Order from Amazon:

>Paperback: ISBN 978-1-910542-40-8
eBook: ISBN 978-1-910542-41-5

LIKE TO READ MORE WORK LIKE THIS?

Then sign up to our mailing list and download our free collection of short stories, *Magnetism*. Sign up now to receive this free e-book and also to find out about all of our new publications and offers.

Sign up here:
http://eepurl.com/gbpdVz

PLEASE LEAVE A REVIEW

Reviews are so important to writers. Please take the time to review this book. A couple of lines is fine.

Reviews help the book to become more visible to buyers. Retailers will promote books with multiple reviews.

This in turn helps us to sell more books… And then we can afford to publish more books like this one.

Leaving a review is very easy. Go to https://smarturl.it/mhgyjn, scroll down the left-hand side of the Amazon page and click on the "Write a customer review" button.

OTHER PUBLICATIONS BY BRIDGE HOUSE

Whisky for Breakfast

by Christopher P. Mooney

The thirty-five stories in Mooney's debut are dominated by a cast of characters who colour outside of society's lines. They are hustlers, prostitutes, addicts, gangsters, killers, thieves, beasts. They are the dangerous, the lost, the lonely, the sick, the suicidal, the broken-hearted. Men and women, defeated by life. Their depravity is real, yet the writing in this uncompromising collection of transgressive fiction, always carefully crafted, evokes the sense that their humanity is not yet lost. In *Whisky for Breakfast*, nothing is off limits.

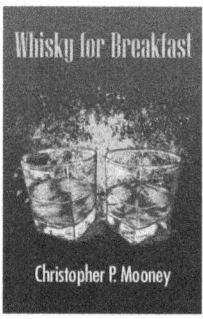

"A terrific read, often shocking and full of memorable characters. This is an excellent collection of short stories and would highly recommend." (*Amazon*)

Order from Amazon:

Paperback: ISBN 978-1-907335-89-1
eBook: ISBN 978-1-907335-90-7

In Fields of Butterfly Flames

by Steve Wade

Ostracised by betrayal, isolated through indifference, gutted
with guilt, or suffering from loss, the characters in these
twenty-two stories are fractured and broken, some irreparably.
In their struggle for acceptance, and their desperate search for
meaning, they deny the past. Some abandon responsibility,
others are running from something or someone. Some flee their
homes and their homelands, while others return home, only to
find themselves even more marginalized and estranged.

"It's not too often when a book can make you physically react
to the words. Haven't read anything as visceral, gripping and
real as this in a long time... Highly recommend!" (*Amazon*)

Order from Amazon:

Paperback: ISBN 978-1-907335-87-7
eBook: ISBN 978-1-907335-88-4

Matters of Life and Death

by Philip M Stuckey

Matters of Life and Death is a collection of stories that
examines, in different ways, the many insecurities we
experience whilst navigating our way towards the inevitable.
Whether it is a fear of the unknown, the burden of loss, or the
joy of first love, each of us shares a meandering journey of the
unexpected that ultimately defines who we are and how we
connect with the universe that created us.

"Varied, deep and interesting, I enjoyed every story. Highly
recommended." (*Amazon*)

Order from Amazon:

Paperback: ISBN 978-1-907335-85-3
eBook: ISBN 978-1-907335-86-0